RELIANCE TENNESSEE

THE ULTIMATE CONSPIRACY

by

G.B. MILLER

COPYWRITE 2017

GBMSOUND.COM

TABLE OF CONTENTS

DISCLAIMER

Some of the characters in this story are real. So, if you are one of these folks, try not to take it personally. I'm not a man with much imagination, and this is, of course, just a story. Furthermore, the events in this story <u>haven't actually happened</u>...Theoretically! "The Ultimate Conspiracy" simply pulls back the curtain to reveal the times in which we live. ...ENJOY!

AM I BIGFOOT?

Now I know what you are thinking. Bigfoot! Really? Yes, I am Bigfoot! But, I'm also called by many other names like Abominable Snowman, Sasquatch, Yeti, and that crazy guy running around in the woods in a gorilla suit. However, if it's all the same to you, I prefer BIGFOOT!

Most people say I'm just a legend, but I don't mind because people love legends; legends are captivating! Folks enjoy listening to stories about legends, especially when they've been *s*ensationalized! Nevertheless, most legends are based, in fact, with just a bit of imagination thrown in.

For example, take the story of the 'Beasts of Gevauldan.' These beasts were actually a pack of huge dogs, similar to a wolf-mastiff mix. Between

1764 and 1767, they were responsible for 210 attacks with 113 fatalities. King Louis XV of France finally sent his soldiers to kill them. And just a couple of generations later, their brutal story has morphed into "The Legend of the Werewolf"!

Ya know, I, too, have a story to tell! It's not a comedy, a tragedy, a drama, or a historical account. It is, however, all of these. I'm sharing this story, hoping you will recognize key world events, many of which are happening as you read this book.

We have often have heard it said that "time flies"? It doesn't really fly, you know. Actually, it doesn't even move! Time is just a pointer, a place marker, a measurement of movement through space. Time had its beginning, and time will have an end. We, too, have had a beginning, and some of us, very soon, will have an end, but not all of us.

Tell me, what would you do if you found the fountain of youth or maybe a magic miracle pill or an alien's secret to living forever and ever? What would you do with it? Especially if this secret source of perfect health and happiness was totally unlimited and absolutely free. Who would you tell? Your family, friends, people you work with, maybe even your lawyer? Well, that may be pushing it a bit, but you get the idea. This would be big, this would be bigger than big, this would be colossal!

On the other hand, how would you feel if you failed to tell someone? How would you explain it to them?

Oops, I forgot to let you in on the secret to eternal life; bummer!

I now have the dilemma of having to share this kind of secret with some folks who may think I'm crazy, or even worse, that I'm not very smart! Many of us are willing to die for our faith, just as long as we don't have to be embarrassed by it. And there is nothing like a condescending remark by a friend or family member to challenge a person's commitment to their "deeply held beliefs."

Anyway, the characters in my story will unwittingly do and say some things that will change the whole world. Changes come because as we go through our lives, we connect with people, and thus by connecting, we change the direction of their lives and the people they connect with.   This ain't no philosophy lesson; It's just the way it is.

First, I'm gonna tell you about Brian Gregory and the connections he made along his way, which is just one of the chains of events that started on April 6, 2018. Then I will tell you about Brian's connection with a rough bearded storekeeper named Griff Miller, which will be the connection heard around the world.

This is the story of Bigfoot, Brian, and Griff and how they changed the world simply by connecting with others. And I promise *I will only tell you as much as you are willing to hear…*

So now, it's time to go; it's time to…

REWIND TO RELIANCE

2028, 2027, 2026, 2025, 24, 23, 22, 21, 20, 2019...
It is now April 6, 2018, at 5:00am as the annoying sound of the alarm clock shocked Griff to consciousness. He reaches over, flips off the alarm, and sits up on the edge of the bed as he prepares to face another quiet, peaceful day in Reliance, TN. Griff has no idea that this will not be just another day in this sleepy little town. Not even close!

He gets out of bed and goes into the kitchen to put on a pot of coffee. He always gets up early so he can take his time and not be rushed. He and Melanie enjoy their morning cup as they watch the local news to see if it's going to rain. Rain can affect the fishing, which is the primary source of revenue this time of year because the river is still too cold for rafting. Before he knows it, it's 6:40 a.m. and time to make the two-mile drive to the store. Even though the store doesn't open until 9:00 a.m., there's a lot of preparations to be made.

This kind of existence may seem boring to some, but Griff loved his way of life. So much so that he was always telling his kids, "I'm the richest man in the world because I already have everything that rich men really want!" and he was right. He is surrounded by people who love him dearly, and he was raised in a house down by the Hiwassee River in Reliance, TN. Reliance is one of those places that you never want to leave once you've been there. It's like God took His finger and touched the river gorge and blessed it.

What's more, you might say Griff had a Tom Sawyer kind of childhood. He grew up fishing, hunting, camping, and skipping school on the warm spring days. At age seventeen, Griff met the love of his life, and at nineteen, they were married. Forty years and seven grandchildren later, Griff knew he had been blessed more than he deserved.

He often meditated on how most folks were chasing after the things which could never satisfy. He sometimes felt guilty for being blessed in such ways.

And this morning, just like clockwork Griff found himself unlocking the padlock on the front door of the Reliance General Store at exactly 6:50 a.m. As was his routine, he flipped on the lights, turned on the air conditioner, and checked to make sure the minnows were fed.

The store is the only building at the fork in the road in Reliance, Tennessee. Reliance is a tiny rural town at the foot of the Smoky Mountains. It's the grocery, gas station, tackle shop, and post office. You could say the General Store is the town of Reliance!

However, on this dew-covered spring morning, unseen by Griff, a very neatly dressed man in his early sixties stepped out of the woods across the road from the store. He looked at the store for a minute and then sauntered in. As Griff put away the fish food, he heard the old-fashioned door ringer signaling someone had come in the front door. He turned and saw the well dressed man standing perfectly still in the doorway as if he were waiting for something to happen...And so it began!

Puzzled by the stranger's unusual appearance and behavior, Griff, the rough bearded storekeeper, asked him, "Anythin I can do for ya?" The stranger calmly answers, "May I use your phone, please?" Griff replies, "Sure, no problem...Are ya planning on doin some fishin? The browns have really been tearin it up lately." The stranger shakes his head and says, "No, I just need to make a call." Then he walked over to the storekeeper, and with a broad smile, he reached out to shake Griff's hand. The stranger then said, "Hello, my name is Gregory, Brian Gregory."

Griff tightly shook Brian's hand, smiling with a toothy grin when suddenly, with wide-eyed astonishment, Griff blurts out, "Brian Gregory! You're not the same guy that disappeared over there in North Carolina last spring, are ya?" Pointing to the other side of the store, he said, "Heck...I have a missing person poster with your picture on it over here in the post office!"

While looking at Griff's poster, Brian said, "That's me! May I use your phone now?" Fumbling around for a minute and feeling kind of flustered, Griff said, "Sure...Sorry...But...Where have you been for the past year? We all thought you were dead!"

In a thoughtful tone, Brian answered, "I guess I'd better get used to answering that question. I tell you what, as soon as I make my call, I will tell you *as much as you are willing to hear*."

Griff reached into the bib pocket of his liberties and handed over his cell phone. He watched patiently as Brian slowly dialed his home phone number. As it rang, Brian's mind raced to remember what he was supposed to tell his wife, Renae, to try to soften the blow. On the fourth ring, a little girl's voice answered, "Hello!" Excitedly Brian asked, "Is this Marie? Uh…may I speak to your grandmother, please?" "Yes, it is, and sure you can, just a second. Nonnie, there's a man on the phone for you!" After what seemed to be a lifetime, a serious woman's voice answered, "Hello, may I help you?" "Renae…" Brian said and then paused. Renae immediately recognized his voice, but in disbelief, she asked, "Brian?" Following another long pause and in a much quieter voice, almost a whisper, she said again, "Brian? I don't understand; what happened to you? Where have you been?"

Fighting back the tears, Brian interrupted her to say, "I have been in another place…Well, it will take longer than I have right now to explain. I need you to come to Reliance. To the general store. Do you know how to get here?" "Yes. I think so," she replied, "I will get Kristine to drive me. I know she knows the way. We will be there in about an hour or so…but Brian, what happened?"

 "Trust me, Renae!" Brian pleaded, "I can't tell you just now, but everything will be explained as soon as you get here. Hurry, but be careful. I love you!" Although she was still confused at realizing that Brian was alive, Renae said, "I love you more!" She immediately hung up the phone and hurried to get Kristine.

Brian handed the phone back and said, "Griff, would you mind taking my picture with your phone?" Griff said, "Sure, but why?" Brian said, "You'll understand soon enough." Then Brian walked over to the counter, picked up the morning paper, and held it to his chest with the front page facing outward. Griff took his picture and said. "It's done! Okay, now let's have it!"

Brian, wishing to confirm, asks, "Griff, are you sure you want to know my story? Some things can be hard to hear and even harder to believe." Griff stood up straight and said, "Mr. Gregory...I want to know!"

"Very well!" Brian said as he and Griff walked over and sat down in the store's barrel chairs beside the checkers' table. Everything got very still until the only thing you could hear was the pump running in the minnow tank. As Brian looked Griff directly in the eyes, he said, "What do you know about Bigfoot?"

When Griff heard this, he jumped up and shouted, "BIGFOOT! You're gonna tell me that you spent the whole year hanging out with Bigfoot? Where did you sleep in his cave?" Brian leaned back in his chair and calmly said, "Well yes...and at the same time, no. What if I told you Bigfoot is not what people think he is?"

"Bull!" Griff barked, "Tell me this if Bigfoot really does exist, what is he...man, monkey, both? Mister, I have lived, fished, and hunted in these mountains my whole life, and if Bigfoot was out there, I would've seen him by now! My Pappy used to tell me his campin stories about the mountain giants when I was a kid. But every other yokel I've ever known, who saw a Bigfoot, was a liar, crazy or drunk at the time. I'm just trying to figure out which one you are. Now don't get me wrong, I don't think you're a liar, and it's too early to be drunk."

 "Maybe I'm crazy!" Brian mused, "but you did say you wanted to hear my story." "Whatever," Griff mumbled. Brian continued, "All I'm trying to do is tell you I got here today!" Then Brian pointed out, "I guess that the only evidence that I am still alive is that picture on your phone. Actually, you're the first person to see me in twelve months!"

Griff sat back down, shook his head, and said, "Mr. Gregory, I'm sorry. It's just that I've heard these stories since childhood, and never has one had any credibility. What makes yours any different?"

"Griff," said Brian, "If the story I tell you isn't true? It wouldn't cost you anything but time. However, if my story is true, you would have to decide if you really want to know, because knowing may change your life!

I didn't ask for what happened to me, but I am glad it did. Even if the price I had to pay would be losing everything I love most in the world! Sometimes you have to lose something to save it. Now I don't have much time, so do you want me to continue or not?" "I guess so," Griff said.

11

So starting with last April, Brian described in detail all of the events of the past twelve months. When Brian had finished, Griff sat there dumbfounded. When he came to himself, he just said, "WOW! For the first time in my life, this all makes sense. But you have to know there's a bunch of folks who wouldn't want this information to get out! Won't you be putting yourself in danger?" "Maybe," Brian said, "but this was my choice.

Nevertheless, what we need to do now will be the most crucial part, making sure my family understands why I will do what I must do next. I will be taking this information to some people who may not listen. My commission is to take this message to the people who fear this truth the most."

Just then, they heard someone pulling up in the gravel outside. Looking at his watch, Griff noted. "Your wife must be here. She made good time!" Brian and Griff made their way to the front door. However, as they stepped outside, twelve men in suits were getting out of three black SUVs.

GONE AGAIN

Griff whispered, "This ain't good!" Immediately Brian told him, "Griff, don't let on that you know anything. You have to explain everything to Renae and Kristine when they get here. For now, just play dumb!" Griff acknowledged with a subtle nod.

Then he turned towards the men and welcomed them with a smile, saying, "Howdy! You gentlemen comin' up for the trout fishin' too, or just getting away from the city for a while?"

However, the men totally ignored Griff. They were all staring at Brian. The man in charge said, "Mr. Gregory, we have a few questions for you. Please come with us."

The last thing Griff saw of Brian was him being frisked and then trundled into the middle SUV. They whipped around out of the parking lot and disappeared in a cloud of dust as they raced down the two-lane country road towards Benton.

In shock, Griff just stood there numb. Over the past hour, he had seen and learned more than he had in his whole life. For Griff, Reliance had always been a quiet, peaceful place to fish and get away from it all. Excitement, just ain't done here!

About fifteen minutes later, as he waited on the stoop, he saw Renae and Kristine pulling up in the lot. Griff walked out to meet them but stopped just short of the pumps. As they got out of the car, he said,

"Renae, Kristine, my name is Griff, and Brian asked me to give you a message just before he was taken away." Renae stopped dead in her tracks, her excitement disappeared, and her expression turned to that of hurt and confusion.

Seeing their pain, Griff said with a comforting voice, "Come on inside…there's much we need to talk about." They followed Griff inside and sat down in stunned silence as he poured them a cup of coffee. Griff sat down across from them, and as if he were a master storyteller, he started laying out everything just as Brian had told him.

"Renae, the most important thing Brian wanted you to know is that it was not his choice to leave you and the kids last spring. Brian is being led down a long and difficult road that many people have been asked to walk before. He told me of the events that brought him to be where he is now. Although he couldn't tell me everything, I will tell you what I know. I will tell you *as much as you are willing to hear*."

"As you know, Brian went with Walter, Ronnie, and some of their friends to the Bigfoot Watch & Campout on the North Carolina side of the Smoky Mountains last April. Although Brian did not believe that Bigfoot was real, he went along to spend time with his old friends.

According to Brian, on the evening of the sixth, about 9:30 pm, he stepped into the woods to relieve himself and just disappeared. All his friends and the authorities searched for months, but they assumed a bear or some other wild animal had killed him after finding several large and strange tracks in the area.

However, totally unknown to his friends, an actual 'Bigfoot' was prowling around listening to them. This particular Bigfoot had been conducting a search which had lasted many years, and finally, he found Brian, who fit his profile perfectly. So, Brian was abducted and taken to a place where he would be trained to be a messenger."

Kristine suddenly jumped up and started pelting Griff with questions. "Bigfoot? Why would Bigfoot take my dad, and what kind of a messenger are you talking about, and who was it that took him away just now?" Griff held up both hands in a calm-down gesture as he continued.

"According to Brian, what we call a Bigfoot is not an animal. And the few genuine videos we've seen of them were secretly posed by the Bigfoots! This has been their way of getting people to come in search of the mythological creature in an environment where they can evaluate and classify us without exposing themselves. The hairy appearance we've all seen is simply a type of high-tech camouflage.

The creatures known as Bigfoot are not only human; they are actually more human than we are. They call themselves Noaans, and for many thousands of years, have had an extremely advanced civilization far below our own in enormous cave chambers left behind by a global devastation.

They chose Brian and a small number of others from all over the world and took them to their underground home to be trained as messengers. Brian said the lessons they have learned consisted of universal history, extremely advanced science, as well as the current social and political environments of the most influential nations on the planet. They taught them everything they would need to complete their missions. The Noaans have been training messengers for thousands of years."

Renae interrupted, "Do you mean they have been controlling the human race all this time?" Griff said, "No. Oh no…the messengers are thoroughly trained and then sent out to help us understand the overall plan. However, we have always had the freedom to choose our own way."

"According to the Noaans, people were designed to be so much more than we see today. In fact, they told Brian that we actually are Noaans! However, due to the precautions that they took immediately following the devastation, they more closely resemble the original design than we do. Nevertheless, even with these precautions, they too have been degraded far from the original Noaans."

Finally, he summarized the most crucial part of Brian's message by telling them, "Brian told me that we are coming up on the end of the sixth millennium. He was tasked with taking the only solution to the few who would listen, in the midst of those who will not. And the ones who listen to him will take the message to those who will listen to them."

When Griff had finished telling the story, they all sat quietly for a few minutes, trying to absorb it all. Griff broke the silence and said, "Ya know, I think Brian knew that I would be here to listen to his story so I could tell you guys. And...now that I think about it, all of this must be part of some elaborate plan!

Brian knew that these government guys were looking for him, and they were listening in for his call. I also think that everything he did was to prepare us for this message." As Renae and Kristine listened intently, Griff continued to detail all he could remember. However, he suddenly zoned out in mid-sentence as he realized how he could help Brian.

But before Griff could say anything, Renae said, "I love Brian. He's a kind and intelligent man, but he is not smart enough to come up with this!" "Is anybody?" questioned Kristine. "No!" said Griff. "This plan has been going on far too long for Brian or the Noaans to have dreamed it up. There is a level of detailed organization to these events I don't think we can understand.

What's more, I think Brian told me this story because he wants me to help. And I know how to start. I'll get some of those news guys to come up here to cover a story about another 'Bigfoot sighting in the Smokies.' They love that kind of stuff. I reckon folks will think I'm crazy, but I don't care anymore. The story will eventually get out."

Turning to Renae and Kristine Griff told them, "As for you guys, tell your family and friends, but be careful;

we don't know what we can expect. However, Brian is doing his part, and God help him, we should do ours." Griff stood up again, thinking aloud, "Lord only knows where he is now!"

Renae and Kristine were looking at the picture on the phone, and as Griff's mind wandered, he stood up, staring at the sun's morning rays streaming in through the front window. Suddenly something enormous eclipsed the light causing a momentary darkness to fill the room. Griff scampered out the front door, following a second of curious reflection to see what could have thrown such a shadow. He looked to the right as he burst out the door but saw nothing. However, as he turned, Griff found himself face to face with Sada. Standing over 9 feet tall in his bigfoot gear, Sada was towering over Griff. Thinking that he must have frightened him by his abrupt appearance, Sada immediately tried to introduce himself. "Griff, my name is Sada. I'm the Noaan Brian told you about."

"No kidding." Griff chuckled, "I kinda figured that out on my own. Man, Brian wasn't kidding. You're huge!" Taken back by Griff's lack of surprise, Sada said, "I really didn't think you would take it so well." "Why Not?" Griff queried, "Brian told me all about you guys. 9 to 12 feet tall, super smart, yada, yada, yada. I mean, really, who else could you be?"

Greatly relieved, Sada said, "Griff, you really are surprising. Most of my new contacts have a short meltdown period at first. I don't think I've ever encountered anyone with such an open mind before."

18

"I think you have," Griff quickly answered. "My grandfather, Sterling Griffith, used to tell me stories about the mountain giants when I was knee-high to a grasshopper. All the same, I thought that they were just folklore until Brian told me his story. I just put 2 and 2 together. Yep, listening to Brian was just like I was reliving a childhood memory...except Pappy never called you guys Bigfoot."

Sada explained to Griff, "We don't usually like to introduce ourselves as Bigfoot. It's just a persona we have been given by those who have seen us as a way to explain something they didn't understand. However, I had no idea you already knew so much about us or that Sterling had shared the stories about our visits. Your Pappy and I spent many hours talking and making plans about upcoming events. Mostly about preparing folks to deal with some of the more difficult things to come. Your Pappy had a great deal of foresight."

"I know," Griff said. "He used to tell me about you guys and your meetings. He always wanted to see your home but was never allowed to go. Pappy also said you told him that when you guys came back, many of the end-time events would be already taking place, and the world as we know it would be nearing its end."

"That's true," Sada said. "We return now because it's time to wake the messengers up to the urgency of reaching out to those who have never heard the story. Many of those living today will see the end of all they know. This will not be a welcome event to most. Only those who have prepared will welcome the change.

But now, there's something I promised Brian I would do for him. Griff, would you please go ask Renae and Kristine to come out here and try to prepare them to meet me?" So, Griff headed back towards the store to get Renae and Kristine, but they stepped outside before he got to the door. Both of them were staring intently at Sada as Kristine said, "We have been watching and listening from the window. Can you explain what's happening to dad?"

Sada thoughtfully pondered her question and answered, "Your dad, Brian, was asked to take a message to some people who have been isolated and controlled by an invisible régime called the Movement." "Are they as dangerous as Griff implied?" Renae inquired. Looking at them with pity, Sada said, "Far worse, I'm afraid. They are responsible for millions of deaths, multiple wars, and most of the violence in the world today."

Sada continued with his story, "Brian was initially going to help us by covertly passing information to certain people through a network of messengers. But once he knew the complete message, he was concerned with the amount of time it would take to implement such a plan. Therefore, Brian presented the elders with an alternative method. He would take the message directly to those who needed to hear it himself.

First, he had the Noaans inform the Movement that he had been taken captive by them by having evidence planted near the camp where he was abducted. Then all Brian had to do was go to the store, make a call home to you, Renae, and wait."

"The Movement would make sure that government agents would pick Brian up and take him to the closest secure location to Reliance…Oak Ridge, TN. Therefore, the Movement would unwittingly deliver Brian to a place where his statement would be directly broadcast to the exact people the Noaans were trying to reach. Brian's plan was simple and elegant, but also extremely dangerous!"

Renae said, "So what you're saying is, Brian, is in danger because of what he wants to say to these people?" "Yes," Sada answered, "But there's something else that you may not have been aware of. When Brian came to Noa, his heart had already been damaged by years of oxygen deprivation due to sleep apnea. We could have repaired the damage, but he refused. Brian was afraid that you would never know what happened to him if he died during the procedure. If he had remained on the surface, he probably would not have been alive today. However, in Noa, the high-pressure atmosphere with its increased oxygen levels stemmed off the effects of the heart damage.   The elders offered Brian three choices, to stay in Noa and live as long as he could there, to return home and be silent about the message, or deliver the message."

21

Renae carefully watched this giant of a man with tears in his eyes as he talked about his friend. Then Sada told them, "Brian chose to take the message. So I told Brian the message, then he told it to Griff, and Griff told you. Even now, as we speak, he is telling his story to a room full of strangers. Brian will not be coming home."

Just then, overwhelmed by today's events, Renae burst out in tears, followed by Kristine. Even Griff and Sada found themselves too choked up to speak. After a few minutes, everyone regained their composure, and Kristine bravely asked, "What can I do?" Sada answered, "That's the simple part. Just find a need and fill it! This may sound simple, but it's not often easy and not often safe."

Then Griff told Sada about his earlier idea of having a news crew come up and interview him about a Bigfoot sighting. Sada said, "I was going to suggest the same thing. What's more, don't just tell them that you saw a Bigfoot. Tell them that you will introduce them to Bigfoot, and they can interview him themselves."

Shocked at the suggestion, Griff exclaimed, "What are you talking about? If you let them film you, news teams from everywhere will swarm this place." "Exactly!" said Sada. "The time for Noaans being just a legend has ended. As of today, we are making ourselves known all over the world. The realization of our existence will set events in motion which will cause people to start thinking for themselves, thus forcing them to choose between truth and ignorance.

There will soon be no religions; there will only be truth or lies. The old conflict between those who suppress the truth and those who share it will continue to intensify."

Griff asked Sada, "When would be the best time to set the interview up?" Sada told him, "Make it for 9:00 a.m. tomorrow morning. Call Channel 14 in Chattanooga and let them know I am willing to meet with them and tell them to be prepared for a few surprises." Taken back, Griff asks, "What surprises?" "You'll see," said Sada. "I must leave now, but I will see you in the morning." Then Sada crossed the road, ran effortlessly up the steep wooded embankment, and disappeared in seconds. Renae and Kristine thought it best to be heading home to wait for any news about Brian. So, they started back down the country road towards Benton.

Just then Griff realized, it was almost 11:30, and he hadn't seen one customer all morning, not even his regular coffee and biscuit crowd. And then, just like the dam broke, here they all came. It seems four trees had fallen simultaneously and blocked the roads that led to Reliance. Then three hours later, all the streets were miraculously cleared. Somehow, Griff wasn't surprised.

Griff's cousin Ava, who usually works from 9:00 a.m. to 5:00 p.m., pulled in, stepped out of the car, and said, "Sorry I'm late, but you would not believe the morning I've had. First, my car wouldn't start because someone had disconnected my battery cables, and then a huge oak tree fell across the road

right in front of my car. I could have been killed!"
She was a little aggravated when Griff broke out in
laughter. Then Griff said, "Sorry...I love ya, cousin.
Let's get these folks taken care of, and then I have
some calls to make."

Once the rush started settling down, Griff went back
to the office to call the television station. He found
the number in an old copy of the Chattanooga Yellow
Pages in a stack of old phone books he kept in the
corner. His call was answered by a very professional-
sounding lady who said, "Thank you for calling
Channel 14. How may I direct your call?" Griff told
her, "I need to talk to someone about a story. A
story about Bigfoot that you guys may want to
cover." She replied, "Please hold a second. I will
transfer your call...Grady, I have a gentleman on line
two who wants to talk to someone about a bigfoot
story." "Oh, great," Grady said. "Give it to Tim. He
has an open schedule." So she redirected the call to
extension 112, and Tim answered, "This is Tim Phan."

Griff starts explaining, "Hello, Mr. Phan. My name is
Griff Miller, and I called to invite someone from
Channel 14 to come to Reliance, TN to interview
Bigfoot at the general store, tomorrow morning at
9:00 a.m." A little confused, Tim asked, "Wouldn't
you be able to come here to the station to be
interviewed?" Griff replied, "That's not what Bigfoot
said. He said to have someone from Channel 14
come to the store, then he will sit down and talk to
them. He was very clear about the instructions."

Tim continued to probe, "So you're saying that if I come to Reliance tomorrow morning that I will get to see Bigfoot in person?" "Yes," Griff answered. "And if you bring a camera, you can film him too." Tim said, "You're pulling my leg." "No sir, I promise I'm not." Then Griff continued, "I give you my word that you will thank me before the end of the day. So, can I tell him you'll be here?" After a few seconds, Tim said, "I will take this to my program manager. I think he will let me come. Anyway, this could make a good regional story. What's your number? I'll call and confirm as soon as I know." So they hung up, and Tim went to talk to Grady.

Tim cornered his program manager in the breakroom, "Grady, I have an opportunity to interview Bigfoot." "Grady asked, "What you been smoking?" Excitedly Tim replies, "What do we have to lose? The worst thing that can happen is I will have a piece on local folklore." Grady reluctantly agreed and said, "Okay, but take Ken with you. I don't want to take a chance that this guy could be dangerous as well as crazy. Ken can check out a van in the morning and pick you up at your house on the way." Then Tim called Griff at the store and told him, "We will be there by 8:30." Griff hung up and thought out loud to himself, "How am I going to explain this to Melanie?"

ROOM 2021

As all this was going on earlier that morning, Brian was sitting quietly in the back seat of the center vehicle, flanked by agents. The caravan of black SUVs made the ninety-degree right turn onto highway 411 and raced north towards Knoxville.

After about twenty minutes, Brian spoke out, "Agent Cartwright, how much longer to Oak Ridge?" In a gruff voice, Agent Cartwright barks, "How do you know my name? And what makes you think we're going to Oak Ridge?" Brian calmly replies, "Because we are."

Suddenly the agent to Brian's left pokes him and very roughly says, "No more talking!" Brian tells him, "Okay, Rocky." The agent's eyes widened, and his face turned as white as a sheet as he stared at Brian in shock. Irritated to no end, Agent Cartwright shouts, "Who the hell is Rocky?" The agent in the backseat murmured, "My grandfather used to call me Rocky." Everyone was quiet for the remainder of the trip.

It was about an hour later they passed through the security gates at the Oak Ridge Nuclear Research Facility. The rest of the caravan continued forward down the road towards the main facility. However, the SUV containing Brian peeled off to a side street and entered an underground bunker parking in front of a loading dock.

A half dozen armed Marines quickly surrounded the SUV. As everyone got out, Brian was greeted by an older, gray-haired gentleman. He was very official-looking. He pointed towards a door beside the loading dock and said, "This way, please."

They all proceeded through a dimly lit corridor that looked like it was fashioned from a twelve-foot, corrugated steel drainage pipe and into a subterranean maze of rooms and hallways. As soon as they got into this area, the Marine escort stopped, turned around, and disappeared back down the corridor. Only Brian, the agents, and the older gentleman seemed to be in the bunker or at least in the main hallway.

Brian was shown into the fourth room on the left side of the hallway, room 2021. Upon entering, he noticed a one-way mirror and seven small cameras strategically placed throughout the room. The room was very comfortably decorated with pictures, couches, chairs, lamps, coffee tables, and a wet bar in the far corner.

The older gentleman pointed to an armchair and said to Brian, "Make yourself at home." "Thank You," Brian said as he settled down into the very comfortable chair. "My name is Mr. Baker," the older man said, "and I guess you wonder what you are doing here." Without hesitation, Brian answered. "Not really, Mr. Brooks."

With a very impressed look on his face, Mr. Brooks said, "I guess you know quite a bit about us, well!

Therefore, I can assume that you know what we want to know." "Of course." Brian stated, "You want to know what I know." "Indeed!" said Mr. Brooks.

Then Brian said, "Today, I will tell you the whole story of where we've come from, where we are in history, where we are heading, and of course, where I've been for the past twelve months. You may believe me, and you may not. I understand because the truth isn't always what we want it to be. Truth is what it is! What's more, the things I have seen and heard over the past twelve months may be difficult for some of you to swallow, so I will only tell you, *as much as you are willing to hear*!"

"That's all we ask," said Mr. Brooks. "Very good," said Brian, as he pushed back into the plush armchair and prepared to lay out a comprehensive account of his remarkable adventure.

Brian glanced around the room at Mr. Brooks, Agent Cartwright, and the three other agents lounging in the additional chairs. Then he smiled a friendly smile and said, "I will tell you my story and answer your questions as best as I can. However, I will only talk as long as you are willing to listen." Mr. Brooks nodded in affirmation.

"Thank you," Brian said and continued, "I will tell you about my capture first, about the people who abducted me, and finally the message. You may ask questions at any time during this process; however, I have not come here to argue or debate. Therefore, I will answer only one question at a time, and I will only take questions directly from someone who is actually in the room...no ghost over the intercom, no prepared list, and no one-way conversations! Is this format acceptable to you?"

They looked around the room at each other for a second, and then Mr. Brooks replied, "Yes, we accept your terms." Everyone was in agreement, so they sat back and intently listened as Brian began to tell his story.

THE STORY

Brian started, "One year ago today, I was camping with friends on the North Carolina side of the Cherokee National Forest, just north of the Hiawasse River Campground. We had spent the entire day fishing and hiking, which by the way, is not my favorite pastime. At approximately 9:35pm Eastern Standard Time, on April sixth, feeling the call of nature, I walked about fifty feet down the path southeast of the camp to relieve myself...number one.

As I was doing my business, I could hear the voices and laughter very clearly coming from the camp, especially Ron and Walter, who are notorious cut-ups, but I digress. Upon finishing my business, I quickly turned around and bumped into what I thought was a tree. I remember thinking that I didn't notice a tree being there before."

Agent Cartwright spoke up, "Did you hear any movement in the woods behind you? And had you been drinking alcohol or maybe taking any drugs which may have impaired your ability to perceive your surroundings?"

Brian noted, "That's two questions! However, the answers are...no and no. Even so, I had no idea anything could move so quickly and quietly that it could come up behind me, under clear skies with moonlight, in dry woods without being detected audibly or visually. Still, I turned and walked into the object, which I assumed to be a tree. A little stunned, I stepped back and then looked up into a small cloud of sweet-smelling mist. The last thing I remember was seeing two eyes looking down at me.

Later, I saw a young man standing beside me, smiling when I woke up. I was lying on a bed in what I thought was some medical facility. As my head started to clear up and I became more aware of my surroundings, I realized this young man had to be almost nine feet tall. At first, I freaked out. I thought I must be dreaming...or dead!"

"Almost nine feet tall?" Mr. Brooks exclaimed, "How could that be?" Amused by his apparent confusion, Brian smiled and said, "I thought the very same thing to myself. THIS IS IMPOSSIBLE! However, there he was, there I was, wherever 'there' was, and all I could do was try not to freak out long enough to figure out what in the world was going on!"

Mr. Brooks pipes up again, "Surely you don't expect us to believe that there is a race of people almost nine feet tall?" Again Brian smiled and replied, "Of course not. As it turns out, Sada-BarSet, the young man who captured me, was short for his age, only 8'-11" tall. The current overall average height of an adult Noaan, that's what they call themselves, is about 11'-9" tall."

"What a crock!" Brian heard one of the other agents say. "And why is it a crock?" Brian queried. "Have you ever met a Noaan?" The agent responded quickly, "Everyone knows that the average person is taller today than people were even a hundred years ago, and nobody is eleven feet tall!" Brian touted. "Really! Who told you that?"

Brian started laying it on thicker. "Who is everyone? Scientists, anthropologists, teachers, and professors in our government school system?"

As you know, thirty years ago in the USSR, everyone was taught that communism was the best form of government. If anyone disagreed, they were taken for an extended vacation in sunny Siberia! Most teachers teach what they are told to teach, or they are banished to academic Siberia. A teacher who teaches any theory about life's origins, other than evolution, knows that they could face disciplinary action and/or termination.

Furthermore, most scientists and anthropologists have totally ignored or even hidden the fact that numerous skeletal remains of humans, approximately twelve feet tall, have been found worldwide! These are remains of ancient Noaans who had come to the surface for one reason or another. Of course, the evidence has been stashed away in the basement of the Smithsonian and other institutions of higher learning for safekeeping. The Smithsonian even has a nickname for them, 'The Army of the Potomac'!"

"Additionally, there is an incorrect worldview being taught as fact by most of our teachers and professors, which even they are not allowed to question! And when your children enter a government school, they are shown many textbooks with multiple references to Millions of Years Ago!"

32

"What's more, despite the lack of evidence for this theory, it's consistently taught and becomes the worldview of most students. This is not education. It is, however, indoctrination!   For years, your government has been teaching its religion to your children in schools funded by your taxes."

Agent Cartwright spoke up, "What about those remains you mentioned? If they have been hidden away from the public, how do you know about them?" Brian promptly answered, "The same way I knew your name, Special Agent David Shaine Cartwright. Oh, by the way, there is a lot more to this story, so you had better call your wife Courtney to let her know you'll be late for supper."

Suddenly the room grew deathly quiet until the muted sound of someone gasping and dropping their ink pen was audible through the glass from the control room. Now there was a thick cloud of tension in the air!

To lighten things up a bit, Brian said, "I'm parched. Do you think I could get a glass of water?" Mr. Brooks stood up, went over, and opened the small fridge under the bar. "Would anyone else like a bottle of water?" he asked. No one else wanted one, so he took one for himself and gave one to Brian. "Thanks!" Brian said.

Mr. Brooks noted, "You are very polite. You have obviously been taught good manners. Was this part of your training by the Noaans?" "Thanks again!" Brian smiled as he replied, "But no, my parents taught me good manners from a very young age...It was not optional!" Mr. Brooks chuckled. "I know what you mean. Please, continue."

However, before Brian could speak, Agent Jones (Rocky), the agent from the car, asked, "How did they get so tall?" "Good question!" Brian answered, "They didn't. The correct question would be, 'How did we get so small?'

Choices! It all came down to the choices made by ourselves and our ancestors." As Brian elaborated, all the men were on the edge of their seats. "Thousands of years ago, there was what the Noaans refer to as 'The Devastation.'" "What kind of devastation was it?" Agent Cartwright asked. "I was just coming to that," said Brian, then he continued with his story.

THE DEVASTATION

"The Devastation was a cataclysmic event which fundamentally changed the environment of the entire planet. It destroyed a protective barrier made of ice suspended above the atmosphere. This ice barrier was supported by three major forces, the Earth's atmospheric pressure, the vacuum of space, and the Earth's gravimetric field.

Over the centuries, the loss of this barrier has reduced Earth's atmospheric pressure and oxygen levels by almost one-third. The barrier's collapse also allowed the sun's harmful x-ray and gamma rays to penetrate the atmosphere where they couldn't before.

Furthermore, the destruction of this barrier caused most of the barrier's ice material to explode outward into space due to the extreme differences in pressure. This resulted in large portions of this minus four hundred-degree ice being drawn back down because of Earth's gravitational pull and the static charge of the ice. The Earth's own magnetic field drew much of the falling ice towards poles, causing what we now call the Ice Age.

Then enormous ice meteors penetrated the atmosphere and created great craters all around the world. However, the majority of the material was blown outward into space. Some large portions crashed into the moon and nearby planets drawn in by their gravitational fields. Even today, much of this "space ice" is still flying around, some in large chunks, which we refer to as ice comets." Mr. Brooks rubbed his chin thoughtfully and asked Brian, "Is there any evidence to corroborate these events?"

"Sure!" Brian spoke with confidence as he continued, "How else would you explain the many giant meteor craters with no meteorites in them, either on Earth or on the moon? In addition, how do you explain the thousands of warm climate animals found frozen solid at both the North and South Poles? Especially the mammoths, some of which were found standing up with food still in their mouths! They would have had to be flash-frozen in minutes by an ice dump of at least minus three hundred degrees Fahrenheit for this to have occurred.

Besides, how else would you explain that organic matter must be buried quickly and deeply to fossilize according to physics laws? Because animals and plants that die on or near the surface are soon consumed by other organisms, The Devastation is the only plausible explanation for the existence of a global fossil record.

What's more, it is well documented that the Earth's atmosphere is reducing, harmful rays from the sun are increasing, and the tectonic plates are still shifting. This shifting is now causing the most earthquakes recorded in modern history, and volcanic eruptions are at an all-time high!"

Mr. Brooks stood up and started pacing back and forth the entire length of the room, shooting out questions, "If this has been going on for millions of years, why aren't we all dead by now? In addition, how much longer can this go on before it does kill us all? And, why do you think our scientists have gotten it so wrong?"

Brian was entertained by Mr. Brook's demeanor as he said, "That's three questions!" Then holding up his fingers as he responded, he answered, "NUMBER-1…It hasn't been going on for millions of years! NUMBER-2…Not much longer! NUMBER-3…Government grants!" Mr. Brooks' jaw dropped when he heard the answers.

Suddenly, everything stopped as a series of three taps each came from the control room window, made by one of the unseen onlookers. Immediately Mr. Brooks said, "Please excuse me; I will be right back." Then he quickly exited the room.

Everyone else was quiet as Brian sat back in his chair and took a sip of his water, and waited. He could hear multiple muffled voices excitedly babbling about something from behind the glass, but he could not make out what they were saying. Soon the babbling stopped, and a few seconds later, Mr. Brooks re-entered the room. He asked for all of the other agents to please leave, and then he pulled up a chair directly across from Brian.

"Brian," Mr. Brooks said in a very somber voice, "We have a couple of our finest scientists who have put together a list of questions they want me to ask you." Brian just said, "No."… Mr. Brooks exclaimed. "No?"

Brian followed up by saying, "You agreed to the terms of this interview. If they want to ask me their questions, all they have to do is come in here and ask me…face to face! If not, I will go on with my story and ignore their questions." Then Brian just sat there waiting for Mr. Brooks to respond. When he did respond, he was extremely stern. "Brian, you are not in charge here! You will have to remain here until we get what we want!"

Brian smiled and said, "What you said you wanted was to know what I know. Is that still the objective of this session, or is the objective to make me conform to your point of view? If it's to make me conform, we will both have failed in meeting our objectives." At that point, Brian stopped talking.

Mr. Brooks stared intensely at Brian for a moment and then abruptly stood up and left the room. Once again, Brian could hear the muffled voices in the other room. However, this time they were getting much louder! Over two hours went by as Brian sat motionless in his chair with his eyes closed.

Meanwhile, in the other room, Mr. Brooks, Agent Cartwright, and the other agents, along with the two scientists, Dr. Shook and Dr. Gibson, try to hash out the situation.

"Okay, doctors," Mr. Brooks said, "Mr. Gregory is refusing to answer your questions unless you ask him yourselves. Therefore, I suggest we all go back in there and put this thing to rest." Dr. Gibson said excitedly, "We are not going to give him the satisfaction of making us do what he wants!"

Mr. Brooks reminded them, "It's what we agreed to. There is no danger and no reason not to!" The doctors still refused, claiming it would be compromising their authority. After more than an hour of these one-sided negotiations, the doctors just said, "*We're not going in there*!"

Frustrated by their hesitation, Agent Cartwright gets angry and starts rebuking the two scientists, "What is your problem? This guy is as harmless as a butterfly, so why do you *not* want to ask him the questions that *you* wanted him to answer?"

Then Mr. Brooks jumped in, "You two have wasted almost two hours making excuses after excuse of why you cannot ask your own questions to this man. Tell me right now! Is there *anything* he has told us that we can prove to be untrue?"

The good doctors looked at each other, and Dr. Shook answered slowly and carefully, "Well…no…but what he is claiming has never been documented, proven, or published in any reputable science journal, anywhere!"

Mr. Brooks couldn't believe what he was hearing! With fire in his eyes, he declared, "If you don't go in there immediately, I will have Agent Jones escort your worthless butts back to your laboratories." "*You can't do that*!" Shrilled Dr. Gibson. "It's done!" declared Mr. Brooks. "Agent Jones…get them out of here!" Huffing and puffing, both scientists were led out of the bunker.

Agent Cartwright then turned to Mr. Brooks and said, "What's going on here? Have you ever been in an interview where the guy answers the questions before you ask them? All the doctors have done is slow down the process of finding out what Mr. Gregory knows! I think we need to go back in there, apologize, shut up and let him talk!" Mr. Brooks just nodded his head and said, "I'm getting too old for this crap. Let's go!"

Brian quickly opened his eyes when he heard the turn of the doorknob. Mr. Brooks entered first and glanced at Brian with an apologetic grin. Agent Cartwright followed with a clipboard in his hand and the same embarrassed look on his face. Brian stood up, and all three men faced each other.

Mr. Brooks started, "Brian, I apologize for how I spoke earlier…No excuse for that. I hope we can continue with your story." "Yeah, Brian, me too." Agent Cartwright quietly injected. "All's forgiven." Brian said, "But we've got a lot of ground to cover."

GOING TO NOA

Brian began again, "As we discussed earlier, the Devastation wrecked the Earth's surface as well as the atmosphere. Almost everything was destroyed! The few survivors set out to repopulate the earth. Most of the smaller wild animals did well on their own; however, many of the larger and domesticated kinds had to be bred in corrals, which surrounded the stacked stone dwellings that the Noaans built to temporarily house themselves. Even though their efforts were successful, the toll that the devastation had taken on the environment was becoming evident in man, plant, and animal within a few years.

Although man's intellect had remained intact, their bodies started to suffer from fatigue and new illnesses. Plants had lost their ability to adapt to extreme conditions as the animals became aggressive and hostile towards each other and man in their struggle to survive.

Furthermore, by the end of the second century, the ever-growing population had spread out and started rebuilding their once great civilizations. At first, this seemed to be a good thing, but it quickly led to a previously unforeseen problem, the loss of ancient knowledge! This loss of knowledge came about as the young moved away, and the elders, who had previously overseen the training of the young, were left behind to help build up the more established civilizations.

At the same time, the world was being divided by family groups vying for domination primarily because of a breakdown in communications caused by an abrupt change in basic languages. The division became even worse as the rising waters from the melting glaciers isolated the continents and the people on them. The new coastal cities had to be abandoned as their populations were forced to move to higher ground.

By the time humanity spread to the farthest continents, the young pioneers had lost most, if not all, of their knowledge of their heritage. This resulted in many of them being reduced to primitive lifestyles and Truth being replaced by superstition.

In a search for a solution, the elders came together to preserve their way of life. Hence, with an acute knowledge of physics and engineering, they devised a plan to build manmade environments to mimic the original. The downside was, the only way to rebuild these conditions would be to go underground.

Their engineers had already surveyed the emptied water chambers lifted up by the massive rolling of the earth's crust during The Devastation. The chambers were enormous and covered large portions of the continents beneath the higher mountainous regions. They were also miles deep in places with few access points, which would make them easier to keep hidden from the quickly growing population on the surface.

Furthermore, the Noaans would have to limit themselves primarily to the chambers for their plan to work except for maintenance and surveillance. Needless to say, not everyone was excited about the plan!

Therefore, those who wished to go went in. However, a large majority chose to remain on the surface and did so. As a result, those who decided to stay on the surface became the ancestors of all known people groups today. Despite our differences, we are all one people.

Over the years, some of the disgruntled Noaans chose to return to the surface. For most of them, ambition was the driving factor. These were the ones who wished to rule over the diminished surface population, and they became great warrior kings, such as Og and Anak. Others actually convinced many of the people, and themselves, that they were gods, including Apollo, Zeus, Hermes, and Thor. I can only guess this is one reason for the government's determined interest in the Noaans.

Nevertheless, one hundred and sixty-five years after The Devastation, the Noaans were well into building an elaborate civilization in their new subterranean home. The first order of business was to secure the chamber's environment. All the access points to the surface had to be sealed up for the colony's security and to allow air pressure to build up to optimum levels.

Meanwhile, the agriculturalists developed a way of transferring the sun's energy from the surface to the caverns. This was so they could cultivate the appropriate plants to produce adequate oxygen levels. Non-solar energy was also produced by the use of hydroelectric generation systems. The water still draining from some of the higher chambers was used to power these systems.

Next, the architects designed and built numerous cities, towns, and farming communities designed to expand with the population. The architecture was in a beautiful ancient design but with incredible technology. The technology was so advanced that it included many innovations that we do not have even today. They also built fabulous gardens and game reserves to house the animals that would be endangered on the surface. They had designed these reserves for the animals' unique needs because of their size, which required higher oxygen concentrations to survive.

Finally, the surveyors prospected many other caverns around the world to maximize growth potential. Noa was the sixth of the eleven Noaan civilizations, Joktan was the first civilizations built, and Jerah was the last.

What's more, Noa is not a city. It is, in fact, more the size of Italy in square miles. Where exactly is it? I don't know, but it is somewhere under the Appalachians, and it is deep enough to increase the air pressure by an average of eight pounds per square inch to almost twenty-four pounds per square inch. The oxygen levels were also raised and maintained at a level of about thirty percent. The temperature hovers around sixty-five degrees with very low humidity.

It felt kind of cool to me, but Sada explained that it was perfect for them with their size and metabolism. However, the Noaans were kind enough to provide me with clothing specifically designed for the messengers. All these things are just a part of the history I was taught in Noa."

Agent Cartwright sheepishly raised his hand. Kinda chuckling, Brian told him, "Dave, you don't have to raise your hand." Dave said, "Okay, sorry. But, I have a question about Sada. You said he was small for his age at 8'-11". How old is he?" Brian grinned and told him, "Sada is eighty-seven years old! Noaans typically obtain their full height by the age of one-hundred and ten, so he should have been about ten feet tall by his age. The Noaans' body chemistry works differently than ours. They grow slower but for a much longer period. Furthermore, the current average lifespan of a Noaan is about three-hundred and seventy years."

Brian paused for a moment and asked, "Mr. Brooks...Would you mind if I call you Mel? I understand that you may not want to be called "Mel Brooks," so if it's a problem, I can continue to call you Mr. Brooks." Mr. Brooks smiled and replied, "No, Mel will be fine."

Brian stood up, then stretched and said, "I've been talking for a while. Do you guys have any questions so far?" "Are you kidding?" exclaimed Mel. Brian said jokingly, "Shoot...Now that's just an expression!" Everybody in the room laughed. You could even hear a few chuckles from the control room. As a result, the tension was gone!

THE NOAANS

Mel said, "I do have a few questions, and I will give them to you one at a time. First, what can you tell us about Sada and the other Noaans...families, friends, personalities, etc....?" "I was hoping you'd ask this question!" Brian said excitedly.

"Sada, now he's a special guy. He was my trainer, along with one of the elders named Yerimi. Sada treated me like a little brother, and the other Noaans treated me like one of their children. I did not mind, though, because I quickly learned that a sixty-year-old man who has the use of only nine percent of his brain is a child compared to a ten-year-old with the use of eighty percent of theirs.

Once I made the mistake of challenging a nine-year-old to a game of chess. I lost...badly! Chess is considered by the Noaans to be a child's game, much like Tic-Tac-Toe is to us and for the same reasons."

Yerimi, on the other hand, was all business. He is two hundred and eighty-seven years old and has been training people like me for over a hundred years. Yerimi was 12'-2" tall and weighed about seven hundred pounds! When he stood up, his belt was above my head. He has been an elder for thirty-six years.

All Noaans become elders at two hundred and fifty-one years old. The elders' responsibilities are to help train the youth, manage the current civilizations, and plan for expansion. For the past five hundred years, they have been accelerating the expansion of their population in preparation for the seventh millennium.

Furthermore, the Noaans are a beautiful people and are very well proportioned due to their healthy lifestyle. It was commonplace to see one of them sprinting across the countryside for long periods at over thirty miles an hour. They are powerful and have extremely quick reflexes. As for their appearance, Noaans dress very modestly in diverse types of clothing, which reflects their individual taste.

However, the first thing I noticed about them was that they had a joy which too often seems to be missing in our culture. From my observations, I think the source of the Noaans' peace stems from their understanding of their origins and individual purpose in life. They seem to know their gifts and how best to use them.

Still, the thing I enjoyed most of all was spending time with Sada. He was my teacher, protector, and friend. He often told me stories about his father, Rada-BarSet. Rada was a pilot; his job was to fly surveillance missions on the surface, usually at night. However, while out on patrol one night, Rada and Raab, Sada's older brother, died in an airship accident near Roswell, New Mexico, in 1947. Sada was only seventeen years old at the time, and he loved his father and brother very much. I was honored when he told me that I had his brother's curiosity and his father's sense of humor.

Sada and Yerimi also taught me the customs and traditions of the Noaans as well as pre-Devastation history. They took me on tours to Noa's power facilities, farms, gardens, parks, and the most incredible animal reserves.

The reserves have every animal you can imagine and some you would not believe. Oh, by the way, Dodos are not as extinct as we were led to believe. What's more, they had forty-seven kinds of dragons." "Dragons?" Dave asked excitedly, "They actually have dragons?" Brian said, "Yes, yes they do!" It was then when Mel started looking worried while holding up his hands and objecting, "Okay. You just lost me! Now I'm supposed to report to my superiors that you saw forty-seven dragons?"

"Noooo, you misunderstood." Brian answered, "I said forty-seven kinds of dragons. There were well over three hundred in all." "Oh crap!" Mel complained, "I really am getting too old for this!" Brian, with a grin on his face, said, "With everything I've told you today, *this* is what you have trouble believing?"

Then with a humorous tone, Brian said, "Now haven't you ever heard of the Chinese dragon wars or the knights in shining armor killing the dragons? Heck, even the prophet Daniel in one of the non-biblical historical accounts, killed a dragon with a vat full of grease and hair! And still, you don't believe in dragons. Tsk, tsk, tsk!" "No, I don't!" Mel snarled.

Brian couldn't help but persist, so he said, "Then how do you explain all the triceratops, velociraptors, brachiosaurus, and all the other dragon fossils that have been found?" "They weren't dragons. They were dinosaurs!" Mel proclaimed.

Brian explained, "Well, I hate to break it to you, Mel, but they were all called dragons up until 1841." Then, while making quotation marks with his fingers, Brian said. "That's when some 'scientists' decided to start calling them dinosaurs! But the way I see it, if your so-called 'scientists' don't have any dinosaurs, and the Noaans do, I guess they can call them dragons if they want to!"

Looking distraught, Dave said, "Brian...I've always been taught that dinosaurs died out millions of years ago." "I know, Dave. I know." Brian said worriedly, as Dave just stood motionless with a lost look on his face. Mel was also starting to look a little rattled, leaning forward, looking down at the floor, and shaking his head. So, Brian carefully asked them, "Do you have any more questions about dragons?" "Hell no!" Mel blurted out.

With that, Brian continued, "Although Sada is not a prophet, by anyone's definition, he is a master scholar and philosopher! He explained that the word *muse* means to think and the word *amuse* means not to think. This is why it concerns the Noaans that we have turned to amusing ourselves as our primary form of entertainment.

The Noaans see our children wasting their youth playing violent video games while the adults watch hours and hours of television every day! He also taught me that taking the time to muse on something truly educational is more productive, rewarding, and fulfilling than looking for ways to escape reality.

Sada also told me that a great example of how we misunderstand intelligence can be illustrated by the TV show 'Big Bang Theory.' Have any of you seen it?" They all acknowledged, "Yeah...sure." So Brian asked them, "Who on the show is supposed to be the most intelligent?" Dave answered. "Sheldon!" and everyone agreed. Then he asked, "Who would you say is the most dysfunctional?" Again, they all agreed on Sheldon. Then Brian asked, "Can you explain how that is even possible?" Everyone looked around at everyone else, but no one had an answer!

Nevertheless, Brian quickly answered his own question with, "According to Yerimi, intelligence is an individual's ability to retain knowledge. Knowledge is the information we choose to put into our minds, and wisdom is the ability to discern if the knowledge is true and therefore can be used productively. The obvious conclusion is that we should be seeking wisdom above all!

Yerimi also told me that you can usually spot a wise person by their humility because someone wise realizes how little they actually know. On the other hand, the foolish love proclaims themselves to be wise! The reason I'm sharing this with you now is so you will understand what I have to tell you next."

When Brian said this, everyone in room 2021, everyone in the control room, and everyone else monitoring this interview had only one thing on their minds! What is Brian going to say next?

WHAT THEY KNOW

Brian began again. "As you have obviously noticed, I have had access to a great deal of intel pertaining to events, including names and locations, which are all linked to what is taking place today. Furthermore, each event had occurred precisely when and where I was told they would.

For example, I knew where to go. I knew I had to call Renae and that you would be listening for my call. I knew how long it would take your team to arrive at the general store. I knew who was on duty and in which SUV you would put me. I knew the names of each agent in the vehicle and who would be in charge of the detail. Furthermore, I knew who would remain in the room when we arrived and who would be listening from the control booth, i.e., Dr. Shook and Dr. Gibson, along with Seth and Larry, the A/V techs.

I was also told of the secret objectives of the others listening in, those who are unknown to you! Finally, I know full well the consequences of telling the rest of my story. I know all these things because my friends Sada and Yerimi told me in detail how today's events would unfold. Therefore, you must realize that the intelligence and technology of the Noaans is far beyond ours!

For example, they monitor every public and private record, phone call, email, website, and com-link, whether government, private, or military. They know which Senate bill will pass, which stock is going to tank, and where the terrorists will strike. They also know what each government is planning to do and who is pulling their strings. They know what is happening on the surface better than the people on the surface do!

What's more, they hear every word and watch everything going on in this room at this very moment. They see you, those in the control room, as well as everyone else who is watching this interview."

Brian then pointed out, "Sada, as well as all of the other Noaans, study their enemy and his tactics. They have studied every false religion throughout time, from Baal to Jim Jones. They have memorized every text and passage of every religion that has been on this planet since day one…and there really was a Day One!

They have warriors who fight and die just as we do. However, they're not fighting for power or riches. They're fighting for us because we are their commission!

What's more, Noaans are just humans! They're not psychics, magicians, angels, or gods. The Noaans are much like us. Yet, they understand the true powers at war in the universe and especially in the world today. They know the truth because they know the Truth!"

Mel and Dave were sitting in their chairs spellbound as Brian said all of this when Mel stood up suddenly and started walking around in small half-circles muttering something to himself. For a second, he stopped in place, turned to Brian, and asked, "What is Truth?"

Brian leaned forward in his chair with his elbows resting on his knees and answered, "Truth is knowing who you are, where you came from, where you are now, and where you are going. Most of all, Truth is knowing the why of it all! With both hands holding his head, Mel asked, "Where do you find the truth? Where do you even start?"

Brian sat up straight in his chair, smiled, and started again, "We have been promised by the One who created everything that if we seek the Truth, we will find it!" Mel very pointedly said, "If it's so easy, why doesn't everyone find the truth?"

Brian explained, "Truth ain't easy! Truth can be scary, and truth can be humbling! The truth may even require personal sacrifice! Nevertheless, sometime in your life, even if you have not searched out Truth, Truth will come face to face with you. You cannot escape Truth. Like I said before, it is what it is, and everyone past, present, and future has faced or will face Truth! The wise will accept the Truth...the foolish will not. The Word explains it like this, 'Because of their lust, they are willfully ignorant.' By faith is the only way to accept Truth, and our nature resists faith. More confused than ever, Mel asked, "Okay then...what is faith, what is the Word, and how do you get the wisdom to recognize truth when you see it?"

Brian leaned forward again and told him, "Faith…Faith is the substance of things hoped for, the evidence of things not seen. The Word…In the beginning, was the Word, the Word was with God and the Word was God. And Wisdom…If any of you lack wisdom, let him ask of God, that giveth to all men liberally and upbraideth not and it shall be given him."

The room was silent, and there were no more questions. Everyone was sitting, staring off into space as they tried to grasp the meaning of all these things. So Brian, knowing that time was short and seeing that he had everyone's full attention, started again.

HOW THE WORLD CHANGED

Now looking very serious, Brian said to his audience, "Now, I will tell you about the Devastation, what was changed and how it unfolded.

As you may have figured out, the 'Devastation' is better known today as the 'Flood of Noah.' Therefore, the Noaans are the descendants of Noah, Shem, Ham, and Japheth, who are also the ancestors of all mankind today.

Noah was a man of faith who worshiped the God of Creation, and by faith, according to the Creator's own design, he built a 515' boat called the ark. And although God called everyone to come, only eight chose to enter in, along with specific numbers of every kind of beast of the earth with breath in their nostrils. Then it came, the Devastation!"

Mel interrupted Brian and said, "How could Noah build a seaworthy boat that is over 500' long when even the master shipbuilders of the 1800s couldn't? The technology didn't exist then!" Then Brian pointed out, "Mel, you are assuming that their society was more primitive than ours. However, you forget that ancient records document that they understood advanced metallurgy and that Noah's grandchildren built the pyramids. Their technology was just a part of the ancient knowledge I told you about earlier, lost over the centuries following the devastation.

The Noaans call it the Devastation because it is the most accurate way to describe it. The Flood was just the most obvious result of the Devastation. However, many other events took place, unseen to the survivors at the time. This is the account of the events which caused the flood of Noah.

First, Noah, his wife, three sons, and their wives entered the ark. Then God himself sealed up the door, and for seven days, they prayed, worshiped, and waited.

On the seventh day, a powerful earthquake ripped open the earth's crust all around the planet. The chambers of compressed water, which were many miles below the surface, exploded upward with unimaginable force. This compacted water release propelled enormous rocks and debris up through the atmosphere and ruptured the protective barrier above.

Because of the drastic pressure differences between the Earth's atmosphere and the vacuum of space, the ice barrier fractured into pieces and was blown outward into space. All of this took place within the first few minutes of the Devastation

As a result, the atmospheric pressure and oxygen levels decreased drastically. The following seismic events, ice dumps from space, and overpowering rains caused most surface areas to become great oceans. Eventually, the once consistent global temperatures started fluctuating significantly because of the new tilt of the planet, which caused the Earth to have its first seasons.

The floods came as the waters were blown out of the crust and dispersed throughout the atmosphere. Once the atmosphere became saturated, the water fell as torrential rains slowly dissipated over forty days.

Furthermore, the Earth's crust started sinking down due to the emptying water chambers collapsing underneath and the weight of the crust, and the massive ice dump from space. This resulted in the water covering the entire face of the Earth within a few weeks.

By the fifth month, the effects of the water release and the ice dump were so significant that they tilted the Earth off its zero axis. The crust shifted from the rapid water movement underneath, and the weight of the rock above pressed downward. The shifting was so severe that the tectonic plates of the entire planet started moving at an incredible rate. As they slid, they crashed together with enough force to push up entire mountain ranges.

Before, the world had mountains with a maximum elevation of less than five thousand feet. The crashing together of the tectonic plates raised some seafloors by many thousands of feet, creating some of the highest of today's mountain ranges. This explains why fossilized clams can be found on the peak of Mount Everest today.

Furthermore, as the emptying water chambers started collapsing in on themselves, enormous portions of the surface sank down for miles in places. This caused the water to rush in from the higher ground, and the massive tidal surges started dissipating.

The new surface of the earth was decimated. Death and destruction were everywhere. The waters churning the ground beneath buried most of the plants and animals. Over the years, the organic materials buried deep were compressed into coal and petroleum. Those buried shallow became the fossil record. There were also continent-sized glaciers created by the massive ice dump, which covered much of the globe's northern and southern hemispheres. Nowhere on the planet had escaped the Devastation.

Furthermore, over the next few hundred years, the glaciers began melting back, which resulted in the dry ground that before the devastation had covered about eighty percent of the planet, reduced to approximately twenty-five percent.

The flood had also produced giant lakes when the valleys between mountain ranges trapped the water, preventing runoff. Most of these lakes have all but disappeared once the following runoff caused them to breach their banks and drain. The most dramatic example of these overflows is in North America, where a breached dam in just days washed out what we now call 'The Grand Canyon.'

Then when the waters of the flood had been upon the Earth for about five months, God caused them to assuage. Soon after, He revealed to Noah that the waters were receding. And in the seventh month, God brought the ark to rest in Ararat, a mountainous region in eastern Turkey.

By the tenth month, the surrounding mountain peaks were visible, and following the settling of the waters, God caused a great wind to blow across the surface to dry out the land. Finally, one year, one month, and ten days after Noah and his family entered the ark, they took their first steps into the new world. This was the Devastation, what the Bible calls the judgment by water."

OUR HISTORY

Brian looked around at Dave and Mel, who looked a little dazed, and asked, "How you guys holding up?" "We're good," Mel answered. So Brian continued, "Now I will tell you about the survivors and their work to try to preserve the ancient knowledge entrusted to them."

It's hard to explain how, but the Noaans have a copy of every document ever published. However, the ones they value most are the Yahshua Scripts. These include every scroll and tablet of scripture dating back to the beginning. They are detailed documentation of the history of man. Therefore, there remains an eyewitness account of everything God has done on this planet from creation until the present.

Throughout pre-Devastation history, the Yahshua Scripts were handed down from generation to generation, from Adam to Noah. Each generation safeguarded them and added their part as led by the Spirit of God to do so. Soon after the Devastation, Noah passed the documents down to Shem, who added his part along with his brothers, Ham and Japheth. Others chosen by God later added their genealogies, history, and Prophesies. This was not for their benefit; however, it was for ours.

As a way of ensuring the preservation of these documents, copies were distributed to the Noaans and those who chose to remain on the surface. In this way, the Noaans would have them even though they would be in the isolation of their underground refuge.

At first, the chief preservation method was the same as their fathers. The elders passed down the information through oral dissertations. This was the primary way of sharing the information up until the time that Israel went into Egypt. The youth were still disciplined enough and had the intellectual ability to memorize and communicate vast amounts of data.

This is why the written Word, as we know it, was not as essential for them to pass along the information. This could also be one of the reasons that God referred to himself as the God of Abraham, Isaac, and Jacob, who were the last in the line of ancient elders.

On the other hand, following the people of Israel's time in Egypt, their knowledge, learning abilities, and lifespans had all diminished. This was mainly due to the environment, but also because of their lack of training. Foreknowing this, God had prepared a way to pass the documents down to His people in a form that could be easily understood and dispersed worldwide.

To begin this process, God chose Moses to be His first messenger. Consequently, during his exile to Midian from Egypt, God called Moses to record the story of His servant, Job, through the guidance of the Holy Spirit. Soon after, Moses compiled the historic scripts written and passed down from Adam to Jacob into the Book of Genesis.

God's servants have recorded their history and His plan for humanity through the years. This was to help us prepare for His visitation and return. As a result, the documents of the Bible were delivered to man and Noaans alike. Therefore, God preserved His word throughout all generations, just as He had promised.

However, in the shadows, those who wished to deceive and confuse humanity for their own benefit have produced Many counterfeits and forgeries. This is the actual motive and method behind the work of the enemy! Nevertheless, even though these corrupted documents have deceived many, the Truth has always triumphed because God said it would.

In a message to the early church, as the New Testament was being written, Paul warned us about those who would paraphrase the writings in a way that would change the true meaning of the message. For example, in the early 300's Emperor Constantine contracted Eusebius of Nicomedia to produce fifty copies of the Old and New Testaments for the church he was setting up in Rome. However, through much persecution, the true message endured. This is how we can know that the Bible is not only wholly true, but it is scientifically accurate in every way.

With man, talk is cheap. However, when God speaks, the worlds come into existence, life springs up from nothing, blind men see, lame men walk, and dead men are raised to life. Even the definition of the word Universe means (Uni) Single, (Verse) Spoken Word. God said, "Let There Be," and there was.

Furthermore, it was only logical that the Creator of the whole universe would provide His creation with His Word. Therefore, He provided them with an owner's manual to tell them how to live the best life they can and then someone to fix them when they are broken! And so, He did."

Now turning his attention to the agents, Brian said, "Before I conclude my story, I want to go on record to thank Special Agent Dave Cartwright and Mr. Mel Brooks for their kindness, honesty, and attention. I also want to go on record to say that when I finish sharing my story with these gentlemen today, I will never share it again."

Flabbergasted, Mel interrupts, "What do you mean that you will never share your story again?" Dave was just sitting there, curiously awaiting the answer, when Brian calmly said, "This is my choice. It is the way it is." Mel stood up, turned around a couple of times as if he didn't know which way he wanted to go! While he was doing this, Dave and Brian watched and waited to hear what he was thinking. He finally turned towards Brian and said, "Brian, earlier today, Dave asked me to tell him what was going on here." Mel turned and looked directly at Dave and said, "Agent Cartwright, I have no idea!"

Then while walking around the room, flapping his arms in the air, Mel ranted, "This has been the most confusing interview that I've ever conducted, and I've been doing this for over twenty-five years!" He turned back to face Brian and pointed out, "I do understand what you are saying and why you have so many people worried. The things you have told us today go against the belief system of some powerful people, some of whom will do almost anything to stop you from telling anyone else! The Noaans must have warned you about this!"

"They did," Brian answered. "But do you think I could've kept all of this to myself?" Now, as Mel was pondering the question, Dave suddenly spoke up! "What on earth were the Noaans thinking putting you in this situation? How can a people who claim to be so noble make you give up everything and endanger yourself like this? For a message? Even a message like this?"

Brian walked over to Dave and put his hand on his shoulder, and said, "They didn't make me. I could have returned to my family and my old way of life if I had agreed to never tell anyone what I knew. Agreeing to tell this story was my decision. It was also the final test of my training...to choose. So, I did! This was my choice and my choice alone. I chose to serve something bigger than myself, something bigger than anything! Besides, I want everyone to know the Truth!"

 "But you said that you would never tell this story again," Mel mumbled aloud to himself. Brian leaned over and quietly told him. "Yes, Mel, I did! What's more, there's something you should know before I continue. The final part of this message may be dangerous for you to hear as well. Therefore, I will only tell you *as much as you are willing to hear*!"

THE MOVEMENT

Brian went straight to it. "This part of the message from the Noaans is about the worldwide political strategy to globalize the planet's governments. The work of the Movement has been going on for hundreds of years. But it has gained a significant amount of traction in the past twenty years. Furthermore, the Movement has almost succeeded in three of its primary goals.

Their First Goal is to strategically destabilize countries' governments that believe in national sovereignty. National sovereignty opposes the Movement's efforts to transfer the governing authority of a country away from the elected leadership and to a central committee or governing body assigned by them.

They started the process by victimizing minority people groups while at the same time pretending to represent their interests. This dual role was effective in exciting the groups to first protest and then rise up against their elected leadership.

The eventual result would strip the people of their right to govern themselves and reduce them from individuals into victim groups who depend on the government to provide for their every need. By replacing opportunity with dependence, the government will then decide themselves what the people need!

The Movement will also plan and execute multiple terrorist attacks, which they will use to establish fear and prejudice in the population. This fear and prejudice will produce a house divided against itself by race and religion, making the government appear as the only source of security.

Finally, they will infiltrate and monopolize the media, both conservative and liberal alike. Once achieved, the Movement will get both sides to divide the people by pitting them against one another, thus breaking down all forms of meaningful communication. The results of this will foster distrust in the media and devalue freedom of speech. When the freedom of speech is gone, the Movement can dictate the information published by the state-controlled media.

When they achieve the *First Goal*, the people will give their governments controlled by the Movement's own special interest groups the license to ignore due process and overstep their authority.

Their Second Goal is to secularize society by radicalizing groups that worship their religion as a god, thus painting God as false. And through the teaching of erroneous science as fact, the Movement will deceive the world's youth into believing that there is no truth. Therefore, when the *Second Goal* is achieved, the world's future leaders will trust the government instead of God, and the government will become their god.

Their Third Goal will be to control the now cynical, atheistic, oppressed, and fearful peoples of the world who have been preconditioned to look to their governments to solve all of their problems. The next logical step will be to bring the world's governments into a cooperative, which would quickly evolve into a One World Government.

When the Movement achieves all three of its goals, the new One World Government will establish laws to regulate all freedoms, including ownership rights, freedom of the press, and religion. The people of faith will suffer the worst persecution imaginable because the rest of the world will consider them to be dissidents.

The Noaans, as well as the other Bible-believing peoples, have intensively studied the scriptures. They know that the prophecies of the Bible about the rise and fall of the empires and kingdoms of the past have always come true in every detail. They also know from prophecy and the proof of history that the predictions about the future will soon come true. Therefore, the Movement will do everything they can to stop them and squelch the Message. Because the one thing which is most detrimental to the Movement is Truth!

What's more, the scriptures have factually detailed the creation, the genealogies, the Devastation, and most precisely, the first coming, life, death, and resurrection of Jesus Christ...Yahshua. Moreover, Christian scholars have seen that the beginning of the seventh millennium is near.

Yet many people in the world have ignored the extraordinary evidence of the Bible truths by their own choice. A few of the pieces of evidence being ignored include Noah's ark, found in the mountains of Ararat; the chariot wheels, as well as human and horse, remains found on the bottom of the Red Sea; the ashen remains of Sodom and the other cities of the plain which have been found along the west side the Dead Sea; and the true Mount Sinai with the ancient encampment in Midian located in western Saudi Arabia even though all these are visible on Google Earth.

Most of all, the actual crucifixion site of Christ with the cutouts where the Romans displayed the criminal's offenses. It was found between the Garden Tomb and Golgotha, and the massive stone missing for almost two thousand years was found lying on the ground directly in front of the center cross-hole with the remnants of a first-century church's walls which were built around the site.

Subsequently, God has revealed the evidence of our faith and His past judgments to the world. Nevertheless, as in Noah and Sodom's times, the world has denied that these events have taken place. Most people still refuse to accept that there is to be a second coming and final judgment. Yahshua said it like this, "If they hear not Moses and the prophets, neither will they be persuaded though one rose from the dead."

However, before there was a Movement, before the Devastation, before Adam, before Lucifer and the angels, before there was light, before there was a world, even before there was time, there was the Word. Not one of these events had taken place that God had not foreseen.

He wanted perfect people to share all things with and to love. God knew what He wanted and what He had to do to accomplish it. He created a perfect universe and gave His creation Choice! He did this knowing that most of His creation would not choose Him, but He still created them. He then took on the form of His creation to live, suffer, and die so the ones who would choose Him could be with Him forever.

Over the years, priests, teachers, and preachers have told us that we all shall stand before God. We shall not! I will stand before God by myself, and you will stand before God by yourself. God will accept those who wear the robe of Christ's righteousness. On the other hand, those who appear in the filthy rags of their own righteousness, He will not! Therefore, Grace is the only thing that can save us! The Grace of God through Yahshua. This is the choice that all people of accountable age and even the angels have had to make."

With a peaceful expression, Brian said, "This completes my story. My part of the Message is done!"

"Thank goodness!" Dave said, sounding exhausted. Mel nervously spoke up and asked, "Brian, what do you expect us to do with your message?" However, Brian's answer took Dave and Mel off guard, "It's not my message anymore!" In almost perfect unison, Mel and Dave anxiously asked, "Then whose message is it?" "It's yours!" Brian said. Mel, sounding very aggravated, shouted, "What are we supposed to do with it?" Brian just said, "Choose."

Mel was feeling extremely nervous and went over to the bar to get himself another water bottle. As he was guzzling it down, he froze, staring at the mirrored window. He was so absorbed in Brian's story, the reality of how many people were watching and listening just now sank in. Dave was still sitting in his chair watching Brian, waiting for him to say something...anything!

Brian said very seriously, "That's really all I had to say! So Mel, have I told you as much as you are willing to hear?" Mel's eyebrow raised in surprise, and he replied, "Yes, Brian...Thank you." Brian then acknowledged, "Mel, it's time to say it."

At that point, sitting up straight and looking even more confused than ever, Dave turned to Mel and asked, "Say what?" Mel just stood there in silence, staring at the glass. Brian says, "It has to be said, Mel...Do you want me to tell them?" Mel looked down at the floor for a minute and said, "No. I will say it."

"SAY WHAT?" Dave demanded. "It's time to go!" Mel declared. All three men slowly moved to the middle of the room, and Brian said, "Thanks, guys." He shook their hands and sat down to wait. There was silence for about three minutes, then they heard footsteps in the hallway.

ROOM 2028

Four armed guards abruptly came in the door and immediately surrounded Brian. Dave and Mel stepped back out of the way. Two other men came in that Mel and Dave did not recognize. The one who obviously was in charge said to Brian, "Mr. Gregory, you have been deemed a clear and present danger to the national security of the United States!" The mysterious man nodded to the guards, who rapidly handcuffed Brian and marched him out of the room. The two unknown men turned to Mel and Dave and told them, "You may not talk to anyone about anything you've heard today! You will be debriefed in the morning. Go home!" Then they turned around and left as quickly as they came in.

Mel and Dave stood there in shock and disbelief. Dave asked, "What the...? Who were those guys? And by what authority did they take Brian to...wherever they are taking him?" "I'm sure I don't know," Mel said. "Let's get out of here." As they were walking out through the steel corridor, Mel whispered, "We need to talk! I have some things I need to check out first. Meet me at the Waffle House at eight-thirty." They went to the parking lot and drove off in different directions as if they were going home.

Brian was taken farther down the main hallway to a room with an assortment of medical equipment, including a magnetic resonance scanner. The guards ordered him to strip. Then they conducted an extensive body search and made him stand naked in a small square painted on the floor.

A few minutes later, the two scientists entered the room. They checked his heart rate, lung function and took several blood samples. They put Brian through the scanner for a head-to-toe search to ensure he had no implants. Brian submitted himself to hours of humiliating procedures. Upon completing their examination, they threw him some bright yellow coveralls and a pair of slippers. Not a word was spoken during the entire process.

Following the examination, Brian was moved even farther down the hall to room 2028. There the guards roughly sat him down in a steel-framed chair, handcuffed him to a steel table, and left the room. Unlike room 2021, this room was stark with harsh lighting and gray concrete walls. There were no mirrors or cameras that Brian could see. However, this is precisely where Brian was told he would be.

About eight twenty-five, Mel arrived at the Waffle House to see Dave already sitting at a table. He went in and joined him. As soon as he sat down, the waitress asked, "Ya want some coffee?" "Two coffees, black. Thanks!" Mel replied. She poured them a cup, then Dave asked Mel, "Who were those guys, and why are we being treated as outsiders?" Mel responded, "I was thinking the same thing on the way over here. They must be with Homeland. I think that they think we know too much." Still stirring his coffee, Dave said, "Yeah…me too…What do we do now?"

Mel answered, "I have spent the past few hours researching the things Brian told us. To keep it under the radar, I went down to an internet café in Knoxville and started googling. Once I got started, I couldn't seem to stop! The amount of information available is incredible! Not once in my life have I ever questioned the things I've been taught.

Brian was definitely right about one thing. We are taught what to think, not how to think! What's more, I went on Google Earth and saw the remains of Noah's Ark, the Red Sea crossing site, and the burnt remains of Sodom and Gomorrah, just like Brian said. It's absolutely insane how we have allowed ourselves to be led around like sheep!"

When Mel finished, Dave said, "I did a little research on my own but in another direction. You would not believe how much of what is taught as scientific proof has been proven wrong! However, no one will speak out about it. The worst part is, it's all still in the textbooks!" Dave and Mel sat there for a couple more hours, drinking coffee and sharing their findings.

At last, Dave said, "It's getting late! I guess we should head on home; our wives will be worried. So, what are we gonna do now?"

Mel told him plainly, "We do what we were told to. We go home, think about it, and make a choice! Brian said this choice is ours to make for ourselves. I cannot decide for you, and you cannot decide for me. I almost wish I didn't know, but I do!" They stood up; Mel dropped a twenty on the table and told the waitress to keep the change. Finally, the two men shook hands and headed home.

Meanwhile, back in room 2028, Brian heard the door tumbler unlocking, and four men entered the room and sat down across the table from him. They set several stacks of paperwork on the table, and the one in charge asked, "Brian, do you know who we are?" "Yes." Brian said, "You two are Mr. Lynn and Mr. Paulson with the HSA, and these are my two favorite scientists, Doctors Shook and Gibson." Mr. Lynn and Mr. Paulson never flinched. However, Dr. Shook and Dr. Gibson were obviously nervous and were literally squirming in their seats.

Mr. Lynn asked, "Tell me how you know our names?" Brian answered, "You were listening to my first interview earlier, so you already know the answer to that question."   In an intimidating manner, Mr. Lynn stated, "I want to hear it for myself!" Brian said calmly. "Listen to the playback. I have already told you my story."

Infuriated by Brian's response, Mr. Lynn said. "Do you think you're ever going to get out of here without answering my questions?" Brian looked Mr. Lynn directly in the eyes and said, "No." Mr. Lynn was fuming as Brian continued. "I have already told you as much as you are willing to hear."

That was the straw that broke the camel's back! Mr. Lynn said unemotionally, "So, you are refusing to cooperate with this investigation. Therefore, I have no alternative but to have you transferred to a maximum-security facility for further processing. Do you have anything to say for yourself?" Brian responded, "I will only be going where I knew I would be going, by my own choice. I would not change a thing! However, I want you gentlemen to know that you have a choice as long as you have life. My choice is made. The choice now is *yours*!"

Mr. Lynn sat there staring at Brian with a determined-as-ever look on his face. However, he failed to notice that Mr. Paulson's expression had changed into one of thoughtful concern. When Mr. Lynn finally got up to leave, Brian glanced over at Mr. Paulson, who was still staring at him, and Brian nodded. Mr. Paulson nodded in return as if to say he understood. He scooped up the paperwork and followed the other men out of the room. Once again, Brian was left alone in the room.

After leaving the room, Mr. Lynn and the three other gentlemen assembled in the hallway. It was almost midnight, and they were all looking weary, so Mr. Lynn told them, "Go home, but be here at nine for Agent Cartwright's and Mr. Brook's debriefing."

As they turned to go, Mr. Lynn said, "Mr. Paulson, wait up. You were silent all evening. What is your take on this Brian Gregory character?" Mr. Paulson answered, "The things Mr. Gregory said today have been disturbing, to say the least. Do you think there may be any truth to them?" "Does it matter?" Mr. Lynn quipped. Mr. Paulson responded, "I guess not. Good night." Then, he turned and leisurely headed up the steel corridor towards the parking lot.

THE GRAY ROOM

The following morning Mel and Dave found themselves sitting in the gray room, silently waiting for their supervisors to debrief them. However, they weren't too surprised when, instead of their supervisors, Mr. Lynn and Mr. Paulson, entered the room. "Did you sleep well?" Mr. Lynn asked. "Not a wink!" Mel replied quickly. Dave added, "Me either." Mr. Lynn asked, "Why not?" Dave looked at the two HSA agents and asked sternly, "Why do you think?"

Mr. Lynn sat thoughtfully for a moment, tapping his fingers on the table. When he finally did speak, he said, "Before we get started, I want you to know that the information you witnessed yesterday has been deemed Classified. Therefore, to discuss this information outside of this room would violate your oath and be punishable by censure, termination, and/or imprisonment! Do you understand?" Mel and Dave both nodded in affirmation.

"Good!" said Mr. Lynn, and he continued, "Regarding the claims of Mr. Gregory, they have been proven to be false! However, they could still be a danger to the security of the United States and must be prevented from being made public. The US and other countries have been working on this problem for many years. They have spent millions of dollars investigating the disappearance of hundreds of people who had returned and made the same claims as Mr. Gregory. So, I just want to put this behind us! Therefore, I need you to sign a non-disclosure agreement before leaving today. Are there any questions?"

"A few," Mel said as he sat forward in his chair. "If his claims have been proven false, how could they be dangerous? The last time I looked, even wackos had the freedom of speech in this country! What's more, why would we be spending millions of dollars on a theory that has already been debunked? Why don't you bring Mr. Gregory in here and let your scientists ask their questions to Brian, face to face!"

Just then, Mr. Paulson leaned against the table and hung his head with his eyes looking at the pencil he was nervously fumbling around in his hands. His foot was tapping uneasily. Then Mr. Lynn coldly said, "We can't do that. Mr. Gregory died in his sleep last night."

Dave and Mel fell back in their chairs with unbelief as Mr. Lynn continued, "As it turns out, Mr. Gregory had a case of congestive heart failure which was brought on by sleep apnea. Our doctors missed this during their examination, and last night as he slept, Mr. Gregory's heart just gave out on him. He was found this morning when we were taking him his breakfast."

"That's awfully convenient!" Mel said with disdain in his voice. "What are you insinuating?" said Mr. Lynn. "Nothing," Mel answered. "It's just that you couldn't have done anything to Brian! After all, he has been missing for twelve months and was declared dead nine months ago!

What's more, there is no evidence that he was ever here. Except for us, of course." Dave and Mel just sat staring unafraid at Mr. Lynn. Dave quickly chimed in, "What are you going to do with us? We haven't disappeared or died recently! Quite a few people would actually miss us. And what about the A/V techs Seth and Larry and all the other people who were listening in yesterday?

What if they started hearing rumors of our demise? I'll bet they would all be racing to see who could spill the beans first! However, I'm sure that you will be able to count on your two trustworthy doctors, especially when they are put under the pressure of sitting in front of a Senate Criminal Action hearing."

Mel added, "It seems to me, Mr. Lynn, that by overstepping your authority, you have lost control of this investigation! Something tells me that your superiors will look upon your actions unfavorably!"

Several minutes passed as Mr. Lynn's expression changed from defiance to regret. Then, in a much more humble tone, he said, "Mr. Gregory really did die in his sleep last night. And no, it was not convenient! I had orders to take him to an institution where we house people like him. I already have very much to answer for. And yes, you are right. I have lost control of this investigation!"

"Gentlemen, I'm so sorry I put you through this. You are both seasoned agents with excellent records, yet I was willing to destroy you both to achieve my goals. I've done this for so long the right and wrong of what

I was doing just got lost somewhere along the way. I am open to any suggestions if you are willing to help. Mel, what do you think would be the best way to handle this?"

Grasping the opportunity, Mel took things in hand, "The first thing you need to do is to notify your superiors that you have the full audio and video statement that Brian Gregory made just before he died. Furthermore, let them know that Brian had told us that he would never tell his story again and that you are sure that he knew he was dying. This will give the recordings the validity of a deathbed confession.

Next, you need to drop the Brian Gregory investigation immediately! It is literally at a dead end and must be pursued no further. Lastly, before they can stop you, release Brian's body to his family. This situation may still get a little messy, but it could get a whole lot worse if pursued. Leaning forward in his seat with his hands folded and looking at the floor, Mr. Lynn nodded in agreement and said, "Yes, Mr. Brooks, you are absolutely right."

Mr. Lynn pulled out a cell phone and started texting. He sent the order to have Brian's body immediately released, and transport arranged to take him home. Lastly, he texted his superiors recommending the exact plan of action that Mel had laid out.

When he had finished, he said, "Thank you! This is the first time I think I'll be able to live with myself after an investigation. I will personally notify the family and escort the body home myself. What are you two going to do now?"

Dave answered, "Well...I'm going to take the rest of the day off to spend time with my family. Tomorrow I will go back to work and take things as they come!" "Sounds good to me," Mel said in agreement.

Mr. Paulson, who had been quiet all this time, reminded them, "Tomorrow, there will be questions from both of your agencies. What will you tell them?" Dave and Mel looked at each other, then smiled at the two HSA agents. As Mel said, "We will only tell them, as much as they are willing to hear!"

"God help us all!" Mr. Lynn declared. "We're going to need it." The four men felt their burdens lifted even as their hearts were grieving for Brian, the one who had started all this. They left the bunker with a new outlook on life, with a new worldview, and they were at peace with their choice.

MEANWHILE, BACK IN RELIANCE

Earlier that morning, about 6:30am Melanie, rode to the store with Griff. She was determined to see Bigfoot for herself, but it was very foggy as they pulled up to the store. Still, they could make out the enormous silhouette of Sada standing at the lower side of the store. When they pulled in to park, he walked up alongside the building and looked over the stair rail. He was smiling at Melanie, who was still sitting in the car, and found herself at a loss for words. Sada said, "Hello, Melanie, it's good to finally meet you."

Then he turned to Griff, who had walked over to the wall beside him, and his expression turned serious. "Griff, we intercepted a transmission from Oak Ridge this morning. Brian passed away in his sleep last night. His mission, however, was successful. Renae and his family will be informed this afternoon, and his body is being returned in the morning."

Although Griff knew this was coming, it was still a shock. But he gathered his wits and said, "We have a lot to do, so we better get to it." Sada said, "Griff, you truly are a chip off the old block. Your Pappy would be proud. But you're right. The news crew will be here soon." So Sada laid out the plan, "When they arrive, bring them down to the old school's front porch and tell them to set up for the interview. We will be waiting around back and will come around to the front one at a time so we will not overwhelm them." Looking confused, Griff asked, "We? Who's we?" Sada just smiled and headed for the church.

Melanie finally got out of the car and started following Sada. Griff said, "Where do you think you're going? You'd better wait here at the store." Melanie looked at Griff and said, "Ya, that's gonna happen...Hey Sada, wait up!" Sada stopped and waited for her to catch up, then they walked the rest of the quarter-mile down the road to the old school together. Ava slowly stuck her head out the store's front door and said very softly, "I'll just wait here." Then she carefully closed the door.

Griff went over to the stair rail and sat on it with his feet resting on the bottom rail. It was about 8:05 when he saw the Channel 14 news van coming around the bend. As they pulled up into the lot, Griff stood up with his hands in his front pockets. Tim Phan got out of the passenger side, and then he and the driver headed towards the back of the van. The driver's name was Ken Starr. Ken was a cameraman who had worked for Channel 14 for over twenty-six years and was soon to retire. Ken grabbed his camera equipment, handed Tim a wireless microphone, and they headed in Griff's direction.

"Mr. Miller?" Tim asked. Griff acknowledged with a nod. Then Tim continued, "This is a beautiful place; I don't think I've been here before. My name is Tim Phan. I will be asking you some questions, and then I want you to tell me the story about seeing Bigfoot. Did you want to do this interview in the store or out here?" Griff said, "We will be doing it at the old school, just down there. We can walk, that will allow me to fill you in on what to expect, but your cameraman may want to drive down so he won't have to lug all that equipment." Tim said, "Might as well; we've come this far. Hey Ken, we're going to walk, but you go ahead and pull the van down to that old building."

Tim continued, "Okay, Mr. Miller, how's this going to work? What's the story about Bigfoot?" Griff said, "First of all, Tim, call me Griff. We aren't very formal around here. What's more, I'm not the one being interviewed; Bigfoot is. And how's this going to work? Your guess is as good as mine, but we'll both know soon enough. Let's go down, sit on the porch, and wait." "Okay," Tim said. "How many times have you talked to Bigfoot?" "Twice," Griff replied, "The first time was yesterday and then again this morning. His name is Sada, and he looks pretty scary at first, but he's a good guy. Well, I'll let him explain." Then Tim asked, "How long do you think we will have to wait?" Griff told him, "Not long; when you get set up, he will show up."

Tim chose to stand in the front yard with the old school as a background. Ken got set up and started shooting. Tim told him, "Let's go ahead and shoot the intro. 4 3 2...Hello, this is Tim Phan on location in Reliance, TN." About that time, he noticed that Ken had lowered his camera, just standing with his mouth hanging open. Tim asked, "What are you doing?" He turned to see what in the world could have paralyzed his veteran cameraman and instantly found himself paralyzed as well. Standing with Griff by the southeast corner of the church was Sada, who dwarfed 6'2" Griff, and standing behind Sada was Yerimi, who dwarfed 8'11" Sada! Ken finally mustered the courage to ask them if it would be okay to video them, and Yerimi told him, "Yes, this is why we came." Then Sada said, "It would probably be better if we go sit beside the river behind the church...less obvious."

The Noaans were dressed in loose-fitting clothes made of incredibly soft material, and their feet were bare. As they turned and strolled down to the river, Griff, Tim, and Ken had difficulty keeping up with Yerimi. His strides were so long that even walking slowly, he covered a lot of ground. When they got to the back of the church, Griff saw Melanie sitting there with the biggest smile he'd ever seen on her face. She said teasingly, "We have had some very interesting conversation." "I bet!" Griff quipped.

They all sat down on the grass as Tim said, "There is something obviously very profound happening here today, and I don't even know what questions to ask. With a comforting look in his eyes, Yerimi said, "Tim, a message is being sent out today all over the world which will bring comfort to some and chaos to others. Because you have accepted Griff's invitation, you now have the option to become a messenger. But if you choose to, it would require about three months of isolated training in a place that most of the world doesn't know exists. However, we have evaluated your background, and with your education and upbringing, you would do well."

Yerimi continued, "And Ken...you have spent most of your life videoing other people's adventures. I would like to offer you the adventure of ten lifetimes. The things you would see and document have been seen by few on the surface. I give you my word; it will not disappoint."

Tim's training told him to be cautious, but then, look who he was talking to! Tim was young and single with no real ties except for his career. In contrast, Ken was nearing retirement, he had lost his only son in Afghanistan, and his wife passed away two years before. Neither one had any reason not to go, so they looked at each other and said at the same time, "I'm going!"

Griff then said to Sada, "Can I go?" Sada looked at Melanie, and she said, "Please let him go, just for a while. His Pappy never got to. I don't want him to miss out too." Sada looked at Yerimi, and he nodded, "Okay, but only for a couple of days."

Then Ken asked an important question. "How do we explain our disappearance? They will come looking for us, and what will they think when they find the van deserted? They will want to know where we went." "I'm gonna tell them Bigfoot took you." Melanie said, "I mean...how could they prove me wrong?"

"I see why you married her," Sada said. Then he told the three men, "Your disappearance has always been a part of the plan. It's what will give your story credibility. Every news agency in the country will be crawling over each other to be the first to interview you. The True Story of Bigfoot! We will teach you what to say and how to say it." "Sounds like a party to me!" Griff howled.

GOING TO NOA...AGAIN

Melanie kissed Griff and told him that she would be praying for him. Then Yerimi, Sada, Griff, Tim, and Ken walked up a path just across the road and headed up a steep embankment. Yerimi and Sada had to help the other men because of the strenuous climb. When they neared the top of the ridge, they came to a huge boulder that must have weighed a hundred tons. As soon as Sada touched its side, it quietly and smoothly rose up, revealing a path to a cylindrical chamber underneath. Sada said, "Well, gentlemen, here we go," and they all stepped into the chamber.

The chamber was a lift designed to transport supplies and personnel to and from Noa.

Yerimi told them, "Gentlemen, we are descending approximately three miles to the southeast chamber of Noa, which is a botanical garden community. Noa covers almost 117,000 square miles and is slightly larger than Italy. It has some chambers with ceilings over a mile in height. Noa's civilizations consist of 242 cities, farming communities, industrial centers, and nature reserves. Noa is one of eleven Noaan civilizations and has a population of over seventy million. Your training will cover everything you want to know, and we will tell you as much as you are willing to hear."

Tim noted, "Why does the elevator seem to periodically speed up and then slow down?" Yerimi explained, "The lift changes speed to acclimate us to the change in altitude, air pressure, and oxygen levels. We must slow our descent periodically to prevent us from passing out. By the time we reach the Noa level, you will notice an improvement in the oxygenation of your blood, which will manifest itself as a surge in energy. Don't worry about the feeling. You'll get used to it, and eventually, you will appreciate the health benefits." As soon as Yerimi said this, they felt a slight G-force caused by the elevator rapidly slowing to a stop. The door opened, and a rush of the sweetest, freshest air rushed in. Everyone in the lift, at the same time, breathed in a huge breath of the excellent atmosphere. Tim felt a little dizzy for a second but quickly recovered and said, "I feel like I could run for miles!" Yerimi looked at Sada and said. "It never gets old."

As they were exiting the lift, Sada told them, "Although this atmosphere is good for you, you must not stay down here too long. If your body gets overly used to this environment, it can make it more difficult to return to the conditions on the surface. Even Noaans have difficulty when we stay on the surface too long. It's like a type of altitude sickness. This could be what caused Brian's heart to succumb to his sleep apnea problems so quickly." Then Griff asked, "The time we are going to spend down here won't hurt us, will it?" "No," Sada assured him. "You may even return to the surface in better condition." "Cool!" Griff said.

Walking down a short corridor, they found themselves on a stone ledge that had been converted into a walkway. This walkway was about two hundred feet above the nearest section of the chamber's floor. This chamber was enormous and looked to be many miles across, but it was difficult to see because of a fine mist that filled the air. A gentle light was slowly moving in gentle waves throughout the chamber, which gave them the feeling of being underwater. It would be impossible to describe in words how beautiful this area was.

Tim asked, "What kind of plants are these? I've never seen anything like them." Yerimi told him, "Most of the plants in Noa originated with the seed store which Noah and his sons stored on the Ark. The rest have been transplanted from the surface over the years. Actually, they are just variations of what you see on the surface, only they have benefitted from the protective environment. The vines that cover most of the walls in this particular chamber are just kudzu." Griff said, "I've never seen kudzu with leaves three feet across, and what are those plants with the big green balls on them?" Shaking his head and laughing, Sada said, "Grapes." Yerimi said, "I'm sorry, but we have to keep moving. We still have a ways to go."

Looking at his equipment with concern, Ken finally spoke up, "I'm afraid this moisture is going to ruin my camera. We will need to video all this, or no one is going to believe us when we get back." Yerimi assured him, "You don't have to worry about your equipment. We have prepared a much more advanced system that will allow you to broadcast directly to your station while you are here. Furthermore, you can take it with you when you leave. I think you're going to like it." Wordless, Ken just stood there in disbelief.

Sada started explaining the itinerary, "First, we will be going to your quarters where you will be able to relax and get your sea legs. There you will familiarize yourself with your living areas, restrooms, closets, and such. Then we will give you time to settle in, clean up, and get acquainted with each other. This evening we will dine together, and you will be meeting with some of Noa's other elders. Do you have any questions so far? No? Okay...Let's go."

About six hundred feet down the walkway, they came to a platform on the right approximately twenty feet in diameter with a dozen chairs in the middle. The center chair had a control console in front of it with an assortment of gauges, gadgets, and extraordinary writing on it. Griff went up and plopped down in it until Sada walked up and said, "I don't think so." Griff grinned, "Maybe next time." Then he and others took their seats. The platform magnetically levitated above two metallic rails, supported by posts extending from the chamber's floor. When Sada touched the console, the platform started moving slowly at first, but it was moving at an extremely high rate of speed in seconds. They left the first chamber in less than two minutes and moved through a substantially smaller and darker section. The smaller room eventually opened up into one so deep that the bottom seemed to drop away.

Sada started explaining the sights, "This is Noa's largest community and is over forty-one hundred years old. New Abel is located over two miles below the Great Smoky Mountains and extends from Gatlinburg, TN, to beyond Ashville, NC. A great sea borders the southern end, fed by rivers and tributaries that filter down from above. New Abel is the heart of the 242 communities making up the civilization of Noa. It is here that our guests are housed in special bungalows designed for their smaller stature."

When the platform docked at the guest quarters, the party disembarked into a courtyard central to five bungalows. Yerimi told them, "This is where you will be staying and where much of your initial training shall be done. You will find everything you need inside, including clothing and personal items. Sada or I will drop by at 6:45 p.m. to pick you up for dinner. We will be dining at the large building there at the bottom of the hill."

Griff, Tim, and Ken told them thanks and went to locate their rooms. They were surprised to find each room had already been assigned with their names on a tag hanging on the front doors. Each bungalow was a suite with a bedroom, bathroom, kitchen, and a comfortable sitting area. The exterior doors and windows had no latches or doorknobs on them, and there were no inside doors, just curtains. The ceilings were just thin lattice which allowed them to see the top of the cavern. There were no TVs, phones, or alarm clocks. However, there was a very intense-looking communication panel in the sitting area with a wide selection of music. Each of the men cleaned up, put on their new clothes, and then went outside to look around.

When Griff stepped out his door, he saw Tim and Ken already talking in the courtyard, and he said, "When do you think we're going to wake up? Ya gotta admit this place is nuts! I mean, just look at it! I don't think we could see it all in a lifetime." Ken, climbing up on a giant stone post and looking out across the city, said, "If this isn't heaven, what must heaven be like? I never want to leave!"

Tim asked, "What do you think is going to happen when we start sending up videos of this place? If, and that's a big if they broadcast all of this, the world will have a meltdown. Every religious system on earth will be confirmed as true or exposed as false. All hell's going to break out!" Now sitting on top of the post with his feet dangling, Ken says, "Hell's been breaking out for years. I've seen much of it working overseas. The persecution and slaughter goes on and on while our networks refuse to report it. If it doesn't happen in Washington, DC, they don't want to talk about it." Then Tim said, "Well, I'll have some questions for Yerimi when they get back."

No sooner had they stopped talking when they saw Sada coming around the corner. He raised his hand to wave as he said, "I guess you gentleman are about starved by now." However, the men had been so distracted by the events of the day, they hadn't thought about food. Except maybe for Griff, and he said, "Lead me to the table. I could eat a horse!" "We won't be serving horse tonight," Sada said, "But I think you'll enjoy it."

As they walked down the hill, Tim asked, "How's this work, and when do we start communicating with our station?" "The day after tomorrow," Sada told him and then explained. "To generate some 'BUZZ' as you news guys call it, we needed to have them think you're missing. So we had Melanie call your station as soon as we left Reliance. She told them that you've been taken away by Bigfoot. It is the truth, and she was thrilled with the idea."

"Yep…That's Melanie!" Griff said, and then Sada continued, "As a result, when you do start communicating with them, it will already be a big story, and they will broadcast it live. That's until they get shut down. By then, the Bigfoot story will be widely known, and those who want to know more will search the web. Oh, by the way, you will continue to stream to the web in a way that cannot be shut down by anything short of crashing the entire web, and they will try."

Tim stopped in his tracks, murmuring. "We can never go back…They will kill us!" Sada chuckled, "Give us a little credit. After all, this isn't our first rodeo. They will want to kill you, but you will be a worldwide celebrity reporter in the middle of revealing a great conspiracy spanning thousands of years when we get done. They won't be able to touch you."

Griff was still walking, shaking his head, "I can't believe Melanie didn't say anything. I'm going to have a long talk with that girl." Sada asked him, "You think that would do any good?" "No!" Griff said, smiling. "Sometimes I just have to say things like that to myself to make me feel like I'm not completely out of control of my own life."

They arrived at the front of the meeting hall and slowly made their way up the large steps. The hall had many very tall tables which extended out from the wall at the far end of the room and no ceiling. Most of the buildings in Noa had no need for ceilings. The chairs were normal, except for their size, and there were three tall stools placed near the end of the center table. The Noaans were talking and laughing as they greeted each other with hugs.

Everyone seemed particularly happy to meet Griff, Ken, and Tim. They climbed up onto their stools, and an ancient elder named Leo stood to ask the Lord's blessing on the meal. The most amazing thing happened as he finished, at least from the guests' perspective. Shiny steel trays with plates of food soared down the center of the tables and one at a time very neatly settled directly in front of each person. Everyone in the hall was served in less than 30 seconds.

The elder Leo's wife, Hanna, told the three men, "Dining together is our favorite form of social interaction. We discuss events, make plans, and share our day. Our daily service to the community is only four hours long because everyone pitches in and does their part. This allows us the freedom to be with our families and pursue our passions. Artists create, inventors invent, musicians compose, and the old folks reminisce." Griff and the other two men could tell they were in the presence of a people with much wisdom to share.

The meal consisted of a variety of fruits, salads, and fish. It was one of the most pleasant meals ever, not just because of the wonderful food, but mostly because of the atmosphere. It radiated with joy and love for God, each other, and life in general. Sada told them when they were finished to simply push their tray towards the center of the table and when they did, the trays zipped back up the tables and through an opening in the wall. Ken said, "I forgot to put my fork on my tray." Sada said, "No problem. Just toss your fork towards the middle of the table." Ken did, and the fork followed the trays up and through the opening as well.

Then as Leo talked, they sat in respectful silence and tried to absorb all they could from his words. "I was born in the year of our Lord 1643, a little over three hundred and seventy-four years ago, only one year after the death of Galileo, who was himself a messenger trained by my father, Estes BarSet. From my father's nickname for Galileo, I derived my name, Leo.

Over the course of my life, I have seen more death from war than all of my forefathers combined. On the other hand, the past two hundred years have seen a growth in population from less than one billion to well over seven billion. The last time there was this kind of explosion of death and population growth at the same time was just before the devastation, in the days of Noah. That's when the Lord cleansed the world with water. However, it will be with fire this time, and it will be final.

This is why you have been invited to Noa at this time. We want to train you to help us wake a sleeping world from its lethargy, even though the process will make the world aware of our existence. Some will see us as friends, but those in power will see us as a threat to their standing in the world. The latter will not rest until they have rid the world of every Noaan. They will nearly succeed, but it is too late to stop the message that the whole world has already heard.

Our mission as Noaans is almost complete, but yours is just starting. However, we give you the option of going back home and pretending this never happened, or you can choose to stand in the trenches with us. Do not answer now. Sleep on it and give us your answers in the morning." Then as Leo stood, so did the whole congregation. He raised his hands and said, "Now the Lord of peace himself, give you peace by all means. The Lord be with you all." Leo took Hanna's hand, and they strolled out the door and down the street towards their home.

After they were gone, Ken turned to Yerimi and said, "Is there a third option for someone who has no one to go home to?" A bit choked up, Yerimi told him, "Ken, the work you will be doing will be completed before it is time for you and Tim to return to the surface. However, to stay in Noa, you must have an elder sponsor you."

Unseen to them both, Leo had returned to the hall for a moment, and he overheard Ken's story. Leo made his presence known and said, "Ken, I know your story and understand your pain. I lost my son and grandson, Sada's father and brother, on a surveillance mission in 1947. My heart has never completely healed. So, would you bless an old man and consider becoming my son? You would be Ken BarSet, and maybe together, our hearts can heal." Overcome by emotion, Ken had to lean on Yerimi as he asked Leo, "You would be my father?" Leo kneeled down on one knee, gave Ken a hug, and responded. "If you would have me. We can talk more about this tomorrow, but for now, get some rest, my son."

Then Yerimi and Sada walked Griff, Tim, and Ken back up the hill to their bungalows. Ken thoughtfully asked, "What exactly does this mean?" Yerimi said, "It means you will be the son of the Chief Elder of Noa. Leo is a good man, and this is an incredible honor." Then Sada said, "It means you'd be my uncle…Welcome to the fam!" Sada grabbed Ken, threw him over his shoulder, and carried him the rest of the way up the hill. Then he set Ken down, mussed up his hair, and said, "See you guys in the morning, Lord willing." Immediately, Yerimi and Sada girded up their robes and sprinted back down the hill at an incredible rate of speed.

Next, Tim and Griff turned to watch Ken, who was standing with his arms outstretched and his head leaning back, looking up at the roof of the cavern as he was spinning around. Griff said, "If you keep that up, you're gonna fall and hurt yourself." "Who cares?" Ken shouted, "I'm ten years old again!" Griff joked, "You may feel ten, but you look seventy!

Anywho, are either one of you guys gonna be able to sleep tonight? "Not me!" Tim chimed in, "My mind is just racing. I'm still trying to catch up to twelve hours ago. My heart is beating out of my chest, and my senses are heightened beyond anything I've ever felt. I think my number one fear is that I'm going to go to sleep here and then wake up at home in my own bed, and this would have all been a dream."

Ken said, "Who cares! I haven't felt this good since Jill's and my wedding. Dream or not, even if I wake up in my own bed in the morning, I will still praise God for the joy He has given me today." Then they all sat in the chairs around the fire pit and shared stories about themselves well into the early morning hours. Yawning, Griff looked at his pocket watch and said, "Well, I'm gonna sleep in the bed, or I'm gonna sleep in this chair. I vote bed!" Everybody mumbled their agreement and headed for their bungalows.

DAY TWO

The communications panel lit up like a Christmas tree early the following day, shaking Griff out of bed. He put on a robe and stumbled into the sitting room. "Rise and shine, Puddin!" Sada said, laughing out loud. "Ken and Tim are already out in the courtyard. Ken woke up about 5:00 a.m., and he figured out how to call Tim on the panel. So come on, we've got a big day ahead." Griff growled and said, "Be there in a minute." As he walked away, he murmured, "Nine feet tall and crazy. Just my luck." Then Sada said, "I heard that! We'll be in the courtyard." Griff answered with another growl. About thirty minutes later, Griff emerged from his front door and warned, "Okay, if one of you wants to give me any grief, you do so at your own peril.

Sada said, "Ooooo!" Griff chuckled and said, "Sada, I may not be able to reach your head, but I will give you a serious knee injury." Yerimi cleared his throat loudly, "Alright, children, time to get to work." So they all sat down to listen as Yerimi asked, "Have you made your decisions, whether to continue with your mission or return home?" The men were unanimous in their determination to continue, so the training began.

Yerimi started, "This morning, you will learn about the social structure of the Noaan civilizations. Our government is an age-based, panatriarchal form designed to enhance the quality of the physical, mental and spiritual existence of all Noaans. No one adult has direct authority over another. This means no one is denied access to privacy, property, or fair trial, and no one has benefits, rights, and/or privileges that are not common to all. The British Magna Charta was based upon the Noaan Bill of Rights.

First, a Noaan's duties due to the community are delegated according to their age bracket. At some point, everyone ends up doing everything. The only exceptions are for those with physical or mental limitations.

Next, all Noaans have a right to their privacy! Surveillance within the Noaan community is strictly forbidden. Personal privacy is considered to be between God and the individual.

Third, every Noaan is required to expand the community through property ownership. Every family unit receives the space and the resources to provide themselves and their families with the level of comfort they are willing to build and maintain. The only mansions in Noa were built by those who were willing to invest their time and effort. Most of the more elaborate homes have been works in progress, some for thousands of years.

Finally, all Noaans have the right to arbitration by a council of elders for any dispute, civil or criminal."

Tim asked, "You mentioned the elders. Who determines who gets to be an elder?" Yerimi answered, "All Noaans become elders at the age of two hundred fifty-one. No one of this age is disqualified for any reason. This assures equal representation of all Noaans."

Griff said, "I have seen very few racial differences in the Noaans, skin tone, facial features, etc. Why not?" Yerimi explained, "What is considered to be varied races on the surface is a result of the dividing of the peoples by language according to the seventy-two family groups, one hundred and seventy years after the devastation. As the groups spread out, they intermarried, which caused each trait to be replicated, resulting in what is now called racial differences. In fact, the differences are just family traits. The Noaans were never dispersed, so they retained all of the features of all the families. The differences are there; they are just more subtle.

Then Ken asked, "Are there any leadership offices or classifications? Kings, princes...etc." "No." Yerimi said, "People are ranked by their age and renown by their character, not by their wealth, affiliation or family."

Next, Tim asked, "I know this is off the subject, but how is it possible to see sunlight during the day and stars at night when we are miles underground?" Yerimi clarified, "The answer to that one is a little more technical. The short answer is that our engineers had a slight breakthrough in transferring light to the caverns. They captured the light and a real-time image of the skies directly above each cavern. In a while, we will be taking you to see the actual laboratories where we process the images."

Tim followed up with, "But it would take so much processing power to render a detailed image of the sky over a display hundreds of miles across...I don't understand." So Yerimi tried to clarify, "When it comes to data processing, you will find we are many centuries ahead of the most advanced systems on the surface. As a matter of fact, we graduated from the binary system to a polyphotal system just before the end of the French Revolution. In the time and space, it takes binary to process a single bit, polyphotal processes the equivalent of 8,000,000,000 bytes of information. Therefore, the actual processing ratio is 540,000,000 to 1. This hyper-advanced form of processing came about because of our knowledge and understanding of the electromagnetic spectrum. In the beginning, when God said, 'Let there be light,' the E-spec, as we call it, came into existence, and it was very good! Well, enough chasing of that rabbit. It is going to take time to teach you the things you will need to accomplish your mission, so we need to stay on topic and on schedule."

Then Sada spoke, "Immediately following our early meal, we will be going to visit one of our research and development labs. There you will see the processes which foster Noaan ingenuity. So...You have twenty minutes to go to your bungalows, take care of any business you need to, and meet us at the hall. See you there." And each man quickly headed to their rooms to prepare. Ten minutes later, they were in the courtyard and started walking down the hill to the hall. Just as the night before, there was a lot of good food and lively conversation. Then they headed for the moving platform and took off.

Once again, they were racing through another small dark cavern. About halfway through, the platform suddenly made a ninety-degree right turn into a cavern only a couple of miles across. It was extremely well lit and full of machine shops and agricultural, zoological, chemical, and computer labs. At the far end was a variety of experimental water turbines powered by a series of pipes and channels flowing from a reservoir near the top of the cavern.

Although thousands of Noaans were working on every kind of experiment you could imagine, the noise level was negligible. Griff noted, "OSHA would love you guys! How do you control the noise levels in a room with a stone ceiling?" Sada pointed at the gray spots on the floors, and the walls of the workstations, then said, "Those spots are sensors that analyze the frequencies and volume of each sound generated in each workstation. The sounds are maintained at safe levels by simply counter phasing and re-amplification. This causes the sound waves to cancel each other out, reducing the overall amplitude. We have implemented this system, to some extent, in all of the caverns."

Tim wondered, "What age groups get assigned to R&D?" Sada laughed and said, "The secret to our ingenuity is, we are the ultimate nerds. Creating something new and useful is recreation, just like making music and creating art or socializing.

We have few TVs and video games because we feel that watching too much TV is the equivalent of living life through someone else, and computer games replace what's real with the virtual. Every day of life is an adventure if you choose to live it to the full." The platform docked, and they spent hours talking to many excited Noaans about their projects.

Finally, it was time to train Ken and Tim on the equipment they would need to broadcast the first-ever reports from Noa to the world. A Noaan equipment specialist named Dedimus showed them a steel-topped table where their new video and audio apparatus awaited them. The system was incredible! The video unit was built into a headset that looked like sunglasses. It projected a heads-up display with mode, status, and levels onto the lenses without interfering with Ken's line of sight. What's more, they were thought-controlled, and Ken was shown how to think of keywords to initiate each function. Additionally, the stabilization, on-the-fly tracking, and resolution were off the charts.

Tim's equipment was simpler yet every bit as impressive. A nearly invisible, flesh-tone microphone clipped seamlessly and securely to his earlobe. It had micro-compressor and gate functions that picked up Tim and those he was interviewing with equal clarity. Ken said to Yerimi, "You did say the new equipment would not disappoint...Wow!"

Yerimi told them to spend the rest of the day getting acquainted with the new equipment and video everything they felt would be good source material.

Griff asked, "What do you want me to do?" Sada said, "You up for an adventure?" "Oh yeah," Griff said excitedly. Then he turned towards Tim and Ken and quipped, "Goin on an adventure with Sada, boys! Don't wait up!" Sada assured Yerimi that Griff would be back in time for the evening meal. Then Griff told Sada. "Boy, you need to loosen up." Finally, Griff and Sada headed out on their adventure while Ken, Tim, and Yerimi returned to New Abel.

Sada told Griff, "Since you only have a couple of days here, we are not going to get bogged down in details. I am going to show you as much as I can, as fast as I can." So they walked up to a designated landing zone for the FFVs, free-flying vehicles. The FFVs were fifteen feet long with a seat and handlebars, much like a motorcycle. The top section was attached by four slender supports to a nine by fifteen-foot oval, metallic, eight-inch thick base plate. FFVs were designed to carry only one person at a time. Sada, seeing Griff looking a little nervous, assured him, "You don't have to do anything but hang on. I will be controlling your FFV from mine so enjoy the ride! However, we only have two hours until we have to be back at the hall, so do you mind if we go faster than usual?" "Faster, the better!" Griff said.

They stepped onto their FFVs; Sada initiated a com-link between their two vehicles and said, "And away we go!" The two FFVs moved in tandem as Sada skillfully maneuvered up and into the assigned free-fly zone where there is little traffic, few regulations, and no speed limit. Before he knew it, Griff himself was racing through the caverns so fast that anything that passed nearby was just a blur. However, there was an entire world just below them. The rivers, cities, and miles of farmland were even more beautiful than his home in Reliance.

Soon they entered a cavern with lush greenery and crystal blue lakes. It was fenced off in large sections of many square miles, with great walls towering fifty to seventy feet high and walkways built along the tops. Sada's voice came over the speaker, "Now I'm going to show you my favorite thing in Noa." The FFVs slowed and dropped very low into the largest walled area. When Griff saw it, he was speechless.

Sada said, "Her name is Millie. She is a one thousand and twelve-year-old Titanosaur Argentinosaurus Huinculensis or behemoth. Millie is one-hundred and thirty-two feet from head to tail and weighs over ninety-one tons. She is the oldest and largest living creature on the planet. When she was younger, she could rise up on her hind legs and look over the seventy-foot walls at the other dragons in the neighboring enclosures." That's when Griff realized he was looking at a living, breathing dinosaur. "Oh my!" he sighed. "She's the most magnificent thing I have ever seen."   Sada agreed, "She still takes my breath away…every time!"

"Well, we better be heading back if we want to take a swing around New Abel and the sea. Who knows, we may even get an opportunity to buzz Tim and Ken at the bungalow." Griff was deep in thought on their way back as he wished his Pappy could have seen the things he was seeing at this very moment. The aerial view of New Abel and the southern sea was nothing short of glorious. Then unexpectedly, the FFVs quickly descended and landed in the bungalow's upper courtyard with Ken videoing and Tim describing the scene.

"When do we get to do that?" Ken blurted out. "Tomorrow," Sada replied, "FFVs will be your main form of transportation while you're here. You walk much too slow to travel by foot." Griff said, "Well, I thank God for being slow cause these things are the bomb...When do we eat?" It was almost 7:00 p.m., time for evening meal, so they strolled down to the meeting hall and sat on the front steps. Then Ken asked, "Those flying things hardly made any sound. How do they work?"

Sada explained the concept, "The FFVs use a magnetic, gravimetric generator (MGG) to produce a limited gravimetric field which nullifies the forces that pull upon an object such as gravity and inertia. With these forces minimized, we utilize electro-gravimetric propulsion to move the FFV in any direction we choose--up, down, forwards, backwards, and sideways and at almost unlimited speeds without friction and g-forces; affecting the vehicle or passenger."

"What's more, you have already experienced this on the moving platforms. We were traveling at over one hundred miles per hour at times, but you weren't feeling the wind, and when we made the high-speed turns, you didn't fly off the platform. Haven't you heard of the UFOs making high speed, ninety-degree turns and then shooting out of sight? Guilty…That was us! If not for electro-gravimetric propulsion, the pilots and passengers of those airships would have been instantly killed at the first turn."

About that time, Yerimi came running around the corner and stopped beside them. Tim asked him how long he'd been running and why he didn't appear to be winded. Yerimi told them, "In the cavern's atmosphere, the blood remains oxygenated almost indefinitely, even under the stress of running. Additionally, muscle tissue regenerates at nearly ten times the rate as it does on the surface. I could run almost forty miles per hour when I was a younger man. We do not utilize many modern conveniences the people on the surface do because they are unnecessary.   After all, 'Necessity is the mother of invention.' Let's go on in." And they made their way up the hall's steps.

Once again, Leo and Hanna joined them at the center table sitting by Ken, grinning from ear to ear. As before, the food floated down the tables, Leo offered the blessing and then talking, and laughter filled the hall. "How was your day?" Hanna inquired, "Griff, I heard you met Millie. Isn't she awesome!" "Who's Millie?" Tim asked. Sada told him, "Millie will no doubt be the main focus of one of your upcoming broadcasts, along with about 320 other dragons." Griff leaned over and told Tim, "They're dinosaurs. They just call them dragons." Tim was speechless.

At the end of the meal, Leo told Yerimi, "Hanna and I would like to borrow Ken for a little while. We will see him back to his bungalow when we're done." Yerimi nodded and told Sada to take Tim and Griff to the art museum in the center of New Abel, so Sada told them to meet him in the courtyard in 15 minutes. Tim listened as Griff discussed his day on their way back up the hill.

A few minutes later, Sada showed up with two more FFVs and landed them next to the ones he and Griff had earlier. Sada said, "I went ahead and picked up two more so we would all have one in the morning. For tonight, I have reconfigured the link for three FFVs, so we're ready to go." Griff noticed a cobalt blue beam shining on a small spot on each vehicle's base plates from tiny projectors mounted in the wall behind the craft. "What are those things?" He asked. Sada pointed towards the projectors and said, "Those are cordless charging conduits which turn on automatically when they sense a power level below eighty percent. It takes about fifteen minutes to get a complete recharge, which will last all day."

Sada, Tim, and Griff climbed into their FFVs, and in less than a minute, they were descending towards the museum's landing pads. The Central Museum was fifty stories tall, oval in shape, and covered twenty acres. It had to be massive because it housed artwork dating back thousands of years, some from before the flood! Once they had landed, Sada led them to the elevators on the east side of the building. They all got in, Sada pushed a button, the doors closed, and then immediately reopened. The elevator had gone from the fiftieth floor to the first in only two seconds.

"How did we do that?" Tim asked. He and Griff both were a little freaked out. So Sada told them, "We've utilized MGGs in the lifts as well. The compartments move by manipulating the polarity of some powerful magnets. The MGG prevents us from cracking our skulls on the roof when going down or breaking our legs when going up. Would you like to see something really cool? I'll turn on the MGG without the controls." Then Sada opened a small panel, pushed two buttons simultaneously, and they all started floating around in the elevator. He pushed the two buttons again, and they slowly floated back down to the floor. "That WAS cool!" Griff said as they stepped out onto the main floor of the art museum. So Sada pointed out, "MGGs also make it possible to raise the hundred-ton boulder at the lift's Reliance entrance."

Looking around in amazement, Tim said, "Where did you get all of this?" Sada replied, "A few pieces are from the surface, but we made most of them. Just like the Noaans who love science go to the Central Laboratory, those who love art come here. A portion of this facility is dedicated to creating artwork of all types." It would take months to cover the entire facility, but Tim, Sada, and Griff only had a couple of hours before they had to head back.

Later, as they neared the bungalows, they saw Leo, Hanna, and Ken sitting in the courtyard. Once back on the ground, they joined them around the fire pit to share the experiences of the day. That's when Ken told Tim and Griff that he would be remaining in Noa with the BarSets.

Tim was thinking that although he had worked with Ken for over three years, he had never really gotten to know him. Until, of course, the past couple of days. He now realized how difficult it would be to say goodbye, and it's only been two days! Nevertheless, he still had almost three months to get to know Ken and the Noaans. Losing loved ones had always been a phobia of Tim's, so he always kept his distance from others. But here, he had learned how to open up his heart, even to strangers.

TELLING THE WORLD

The next morning Tim rose early, a bit nervous about the first broadcast to the surface; he decided to go for a run. After a few minutes, he realized that he was not getting winded at all. Therefore, he pushed himself to a new level of performance he had never dreamed of. However, he was almost run down by a Noaan named Bart on the way back. Bart was out for a run and wasn't expecting to come across anyone as small as Tim to be on the path. Fortunately, he was able to leap over Tim at the last second. They sat down for a few minutes, shared a good laugh, and then continued on their separate runs. Tim arrived at his bungalow invigorated and ready for another day of adventure.

After cleaning up, Tim met the others in the courtyard, where Griff excitedly told about Melanie's call. It seems that Yerimi and Sada not only had an in-depth conversation with her at the church that first day, but they had also given her a remarkable communicator. Melanie had called Griff this morning to let him know what was going on in Reliance.

She told him how the press and police had all but taken over the store as they scoured the mountainsides looking for the three of them. There were even a couple of black SUVs at the school with the area cordoned off. She said the press reminded her of the seagulls in 'Finding Nemo,' with each trying to be the first to get the scoop! Mine, mine, mine,

mine... Melanie also said she had been questioned by the police and the men in the dark gray suits. They told her not to talk to the press. Nevertheless, the press had already acquired pictures of the footprints up by the church, and there was a full-blown Bigfoot frenzy going on in Reliance. That's when Yerimi told Griff it was time for him to return home.

Nervously Tim asked, "What do I say? How is the best way to get the message across to the people?" Yerimi told him, "Today, you will be communicating with your Chief Production Manager, Grady Sapp. Just explain to him that you will be up-linking to Channel 14 with fifteen-minute daily updates starting at 6:45pm EST. And emphasize that every broadcast will provide new revelations into the story of Bigfoot's world."

Yerimi continued, "He will take care of getting the word out by syndicating the broadcast live, that is until they figure out the substance of the message. Following the first broadcast, you will be in charge of the content and have to decide what to report yourself." Then Sada said to Griff, "We have a tiny window of time to get you home safely, so we'd better get going." Griff said his goodbyes, and they headed toward the same lift they came in on just only two days earlier.

As Yerimi predicted, Grady had every network and news agency broadcasting live by the fourth show. Tim's daily broadcast quickly became a highly anticipated feature, especially following the first show where he introduced Leo, Yerimi, and the other

Noaans to the world. This secret civilization of twelve-foot-tall genius supermen had captured the imaginations of the entire planet.

But it didn't take long before representatives of the Movement tried to shut them down. However, as each network started bowing to pressure to stop the broadcast, the Noaans initiated a software that superseded the network's own systems' control between 6:45pm and 7:00pm each day. Despite the Movement's efforts, the show went on!

Needless to say, as the pressure intensified, the tactics escalated. The military was called to take over the search for Tim, Ken, and the Noaans. In the name of national security, the press was kept at a distance, and although the military utilized every resource and technology available, their efforts came up short.

At the end of the three months, as the daytime shift of FBI, Homeland Security, and the military arrived at the store for their morning chicken biscuit, they saw Tim resting comfortably in the old steel chair on the front step. The store had been under twenty-four-hour surveillance and surrounded by guards, but no one had seen him arrive. The Homeland agents quickly hustled Tim into one of their black SUVs and drove off.

Tim said, "Let me guess, an underground bunker in Oak Ridge." There were no replies, and no one would speak to or even look directly at him. When they arrived, they entered through the same corridor as Brian Gregory had entered three months before and escorted Tim to room 2021. He was left in the room alone, so he walked over to the fridge and got himself a bottled water. Looking around, Tim said, "I understand that Mr. Mel Brooks is retired, and all the other agents have been reassigned. Nevertheless, I would like to talk to someone of Mr. Brooks' rank, preferably someone with authority to make command decisions."

There was no response, so Tim walked over to the mirrored window, cupped his hands to his face, and tried to look through it. "Anybody home?" he yelled. "I guess not…I'll just wait here." Tim settled down into the overstuffed armchair and closed his eyes as if he were taking a nap. Seconds later, three men entered the room. Still, no one was speaking. That's when Tim said, "Not a very chatty bunch, are we?" At that point, one of the men said, "We have not come here to be your buddy, your chum, or your BFF. So, please refrain from the chit-chat.

You have absolutely no option except to co-operate with us. If you do not, things will get particularly unpleasant for everyone. I have a list which you will answer to my satisfaction, or I am authorized to use extreme interrogation techniques to acquire those answers." One of the other men set a briefcase on the coffee table and opened it to reveal several vials and a hypodermic. Just then, a thunderous rapping came from the window, and a voice over the intercom said, "Stop what you're doing and turn on your monitor immediately!"

One of the three agents grabbed the remote and turned it on. As the picture on the sixty-inch monitor quickly came into focus, the agents found themselves paralyzed at what they saw. They saw themselves and Tim sitting in one of the most secure rooms in the nation. This room had been isolated from every outside network. As a result of Brian Gregory's interrogation, the bunker had been set up on a hardwired, onsite server with zero access to the outside, wireless or otherwise.

Nevertheless, there they were in living color. The lead agent demanded, "How are you doing this? This is impossible!" Then an angry voice from the control room shouted, "I don't give a damn how he's doing it...It's being streamed live to the internet!" The agent said, "Can't you just cut the power to the network?" "That's the first thing we tried," the voice said.

Suddenly, they heard a different voice coming from the monitor. It was Leo BarSet. The monitor had switched to the multi-screen mode by itself, with Leo in the bottom right square and the other three blank. Leo said, "Today, the world will be a witness to a summit between Noa and three world powers, the United States of America, Russia, and Israel. We have confirmation that the leaders of these countries are watching this at this very moment. So without any further delay, I welcome President Trump, President Putin, and Prime Minister Netanyahu."

The other three screens immediately switched on when Leo finished his welcome with the aforementioned leaders now included in the broadcast. All three of them had a 'deer in the headlights look on their faces. "Gentlemen," Leo started, "Due to time restraints, we must have this discussion now." Putin declared that he would not be a part of this charade and turned off the power to his computer, which cut power to the rest of Moscow. Then Leo said, "Please be patient; he will be back momentarily." In about forty-five seconds, a fuming President Putin came back on ranting about this being an act of war! Leo calmly told him, "You have been warring against us for a thousand years, yet we have never retaliated in kind. If we had, we would have failed in our mission, and you would no longer exist. We have a job to do, along with every other messenger on the earth, and we will see it through."

"Each of you have seen Tim Phan's broadcasts from Noa over the past three months. And you all tried to stop them with every means available to you with no success. Thus, I propose a dialogue which those who manipulate you and your governments into fulfilling their agenda through bribery or coercion will unfailingly oppose. If this worries you, it should. Because the results of the final battles between God's people and the enemy will leave the earth and everything on it totally destroyed.

Prime Minister Netanyahu said, "So, you are saying that there is only one path to God and that the Jews, God's holy people, will be destroyed by God?" "No," Leo continued, "What God says in His word is there is only one way to be saved, and that is by accepting Yahshua. On the other hand, the only way for anyone Jew or otherwise to be lost is to reject God's Messiah. This message was given to us in the garden of Eden. And again in another garden where Yahshua rose from the dead. Benjamin, although you know these things to be true, you must still choose for yourself because remaining neutral is not an option."

"Next, President Trump, who had been uncharacteristically silent until this time, asked, "What makes you think that your religion is right and everyone else's is wrong? I've met many, many hundreds of good, special people from a multitude of religions, and you're implying that they are all going to burn forever in some hellacious, never-ending place of torment?"

Leo answered him, "God spoke these words, saying, 'I am the Lord thy God, which have brought thee out of the land of Egypt, out of the house of bondage. Thou shalt have no other gods before me.' Furthermore, God said,'...to him that cometh to Me, I will in no wise cast out.' And again, 'My sheep hear My voice, and I know them, and they follow Me: And I will give them eternal life;' Then He bade us, 'Come unto me, all ye that labor and are heavy laden and I will give you rest.' This matter concludes that eternal life is for God's people alone. Even so, our sinful human natures crave the freedom to have or to be our own gods. This is the wide path that leads to destruction. There are only two religions, God's and man's."

It was crystal clear by the deafening silence which followed Leo's comments that the gauntlet had been thrown down. Therefore, he extended an invitation for each government to send one representative of their choice to meet with the elders in Noa. However, Leo asked for one in particular from the Americans, Ben Carson.   Dr. Carson was chosen for his understanding of scripture and especially of prophecy. The final discussions were detailed instructions on releasing Tim to keep him from being recaptured by the media circus that had set up camp at every gate. So, they took Tim just outside the bunker where he was to walk out into the woods about fifty feet. However, a highly trained platoon of US Marines watched his every move when almost before their eyes, he disappeared.

Two days later, the representatives and their entourages arrived at the airport in Knoxville, TN, and drove caravan-style all the way to Reliance. They were to meet with Griff at the store to get instructions for the next leg of the trip. Once they arrived, Griff told them that he, the representatives, and their security would go for a walk down under the train tracks and up the holler past the fishing cabins. So they took off walking, a group of thirty-one men in total. A footpath that ended at a small clearing about an eighth-mile walk was just beyond the cabins. When they were all in the clearing, Dr. Carson asked

Griff, "What now?" Griff smiled and said, "You go to Noa."

Next, a strong voice that seemed to be very close instructed them. "Please stand very still and do not attempt to retrieve your weapons, or you will be neutralized." A couple of seconds later, it appeared that the trees were coming to life, and they soon found themselves surrounded by over a dozen Bigfoot.   The sudden appearance of the camouflage giants proved too much for one of the Russian security team, and he went for his weapon. The next thing they noticed was a sweet-smelling mist filling the air.

An hour later, they started waking up to discover their primaries were missing. Almost immediately, they started running out into the woods in every direction, desperately looking for clues to where they could be. Still, the only signs were several thirty-inch human-like footprints found in the clearing. Griff sat up, smiled, and then said, "If we hurry, we may get back to the store in time to see them on the news." Feeling defeated, the security detail headed back towards the store to report in.

FACE TO FACE

As Dr. Carson was waking, he remembered reading the transcript of Brian Gregory's abduction, and sure enough, there was Sada smiling at him. Sada was in charge of the detail to escort the new visitors to the elder's meeting chamber. The other two gentlemen were Andrea Novacheck of Russia and Daniel Yochanan of Israel. All three men were well prepared for this meeting and expected some unusual security to expedite their arrival in Noa. However, when they stepped out of the infirmary into New Able, they found themselves overcome with the sheer enormity of the cavern. Sada said politely, "My name is Sada. Please follow me to the transportation platform. The elders are very anxious to finally meet you in person." They all were settled into their seats when Sada noticed the Russian representative was using a tiny camera to take pictures without drawing attention to himself. So Sada told them, "You are welcome to take all the pictures you wish, and if you do not have a camera, one will be provided for each of you." The next thing the representatives knew, they were racing through New Able towards the heart of the city. Thinking out loud as he stepped off of the platform, Dr. Carson said, "This is Amazing!"

They were all surprised when they crossed the bridge and entered the meeting chamber to find a normal human, just like themselves, in charge of the media crew. The head videographer came and introduced himself. "Hello, my name is Ken Starr, and I will be videoing your broadcast from Noa to the rest of the world. If there is anything you need, just let me know. In addition, Tim Phan will be available to interview each of you separately if you wish. He will also be returning to the surface with you. I hope you enjoy your visit." Dr. Carson asked Ken, "How do you broadcast to the outside without exposing your location?" Ken told him, "I have no idea. I simply had to accept that the Noaans have seventy percent more brain usage than we do and our limitations are not theirs. This is why most of the things we find impossible to mentally process ain't brain surgery to them. Even so, they too have degraded as far from the pre-flood humans as we have from them. Now, the Noaans are trying to show us how all mankind, who chooses to, may be saved and restored to what God originally created them to be."

While Ken was speaking, Yerimi quietly walked up behind Dr. Carson and said. "But you knew this already, didn't you, Dr. Carson?" Ben spun around and found himself looking up into the face of a man who was twice his height. "Good morning, gentlemen." Then Yerimi smiled and said. "It's time to go into the meeting. This way, please."

Yerimi was one of the younger elders in this meeting of about twelve hundred elders. The room was circular, with rows spiraling down to the main floor. The seating started with the youngest elders at the top and ended with the oldest on the main level. Also on the main floor was a huge round table with twenty-four chairs set around it and one very large chair at the head of the table, which remained empty.

Three tall stools were positioned at the foot of the table for each of the guests. Yerimi stood directly behind the three as they took their places. He was there to answer any questions that they did not want to ask in an open forum.

Leo BarSet started by offering a prayer, calling the meeting to order, and thanking the three men for coming to Noa. He then went straightway to the business at hand, "The Noaans have lived beneath the surface of this planet for forty-two centuries. We have done this to preserve a way of life, the Word of Truth, and finally to prepare mankind for the last days of the sixth millennium. This time has now come.

The planet has but a few years until it is utterly destroyed to be remade into its original form. The enemy wishes to lead as many who would follow into the same destruction made for him. Everyone we know and love will be saved or destroyed on the last day. Furthermore, the solution is not found in the world's riches, powers, or religions. The only hope for the world is found in the one that created it in the beginning. Salvation is found by accepting the grace of God that He gives to all without measure, simply for placing our faith in His only Son, Yahshua. There is no other name under heaven by which we can be saved.

We've invited each of you here today because of your diverse faiths to help illustrate how the image of God you have learned from childhood will influence the overall direction of your lives. And furthermore, how each of you has a misguided impression of the one true God. All religions which depend on good works in part or in whole for Salvation are actually the same religion. The time has come for this to end!"

"Is that a threat?" Andrea asked. 'No." Leo replied, "It is a warning of things to come.   The cup is nearly full, time is running out, and the Noaans voices will soon be silenced by the enemy. We know that we will not see the last few days of this world and that the broadcast of this meeting has sealed the decision to eliminate us from existence. In the end, however, the attempt will be proven futile because of our faith; we will be raised on the last day."

Next, Ambassador Yochanan asked, "Do the Noaans not believe that the temple in Jerusalem will be rebuilt, or that the Messiah shall return to rule on the earth for a thousand years?" The answer from Leo was slow, thoughtful, and distressing to Daniel, "Do not put your faith in signs and wonders, or you will be deceived. Israel was deceived when Yahshua came the first time because they expected Him to set up His kingdom on this world where they would live and rule with Him. Even now, the Jews and many of the Christians are looking for the same thing. As Solomon told us three thousand years ago, 'There is nothing new under the sun."

Dr. Carson had been upset because of the comment made earlier that they all had a misguided image of God, so he inquired of Leo, "I believe we are saved by grace, so how is that wrong?" Leo answered, "Do you believe in grace by faith alone, or are there other stipulations included. God knew that salvation by His grace through faith alone is the only way anyone of us would be saved. Grace conditional upon works is no longer grace, and the enemy wins. Therefore, if you do not know for sure that if you had to stand before God at this very moment that you are saved, you are trusting in yourself and not the righteousness of Yahshua to save you.

Therefore, come back to God's Word because it alone has the Truth that I know you are seeking." Ben declared, "I have always believed that the Bible was God's Holy Word." Now pressuring Ben to face the source of his faith and doctrines, Leo asked, "The Bible alone? From the times of the early church, Christians have laid down their lives in defense of the Holy Scriptures. However, from Paul's day until now, God's word has been watered down and perverted into many false versions which teach erroneous doctrines and other gospels." So Ben asked Leo, "Then which version is the correct version?" Leo's responded, "Look at the history of the versions and the people who used them. The true version is represented by those persecuted for defending it, and the false versions by their persecutors. By their fruits, you will know them."

Looking somewhat concerned about what he was about to share, Leo continued, "Just recently, I heard one of the Presidents of the United States claim that Christians were responsible for the crusades and countless other persecutions. This, too, is a lie of the enemy. The true Christians were those being persecuted by a church that professes Christianity but denies the power.

This false church is actually in the service of the enemy. The bible tells us that in the last days, history will repeat itself. The same spirits that motivated the persecutors of old will rise up in the last days to destroy God's people. The time of the end will be beyond horrible, and many will find themselves on the side of the enemy doing unspeakable things in the name of their god.

From your studies of prophecy, Ben, you know that the false church and the last superpower will unite as the lamb-like beast, forcing the world into a worldwide government to be administrated by the enemy. A new world order. I declare in the hearing of our guest and the world, this prophecy is being fulfilled as we speak."

Dr. Carson knew the consequences of Leo's words and fervor with which most of the world's governments would respond; he still said, "Elder BarSet and Elders of Noa, my heart is heavy because I know what you say is true. I thank you for your courage, for reaching out from the safety of your magnificent home to help prepare the world for the future. May you and I, along with countless others listening to this broadcast today, meet in the Kingdom?"

THE MOVEMENT'S RESPONSE

Even before the three had left the meeting, many of the world's governments were calling for an end to the Noaan's broadcast and some for the end of the Noaans themselves. The media in America was calling for Ben Carson's resignation, and there was talk of charges of treason being brought by some members of Congress and the Senate. On the other hand, the administration had gone utterly silent as they tried desperately to regroup. Although he knew there would be hell to pay upon his return, Ben was at peace with his statement.

On the contrary, the Israeli and Russian representatives remained silent, requesting that they be returned to the surface immediately. Expecting this response, the Noaans had already made preparations, and before they knew it, the three men, with Tim, were waking up in the same clearing where they had disappeared. As soon as they sat up, security came running from every direction. No one had any idea how they got back into the clearing without being seen by agents, drones, and/or satellites. The Russian and Israeli delegates were quickly whisked away by their security details.

Ben and Tim sat cross-legged on the ground, waiting for the American detail. Ben told Tim, "I'm in no hurry to get back to DC. I know there's going to be a lynch mob, just waiting to string me up. At any rate, I'm glad the Lord gave me the courage to say what I did. Even so, I'm worried about my family." Tim said, "Just remember Daniel in the lion's den and his friends in the fiery furnace, God will bless your decision. Currently, I have no idea what's going to happen to me. Maybe I should have stayed in Noa, but I can't shake the feeling that God has something more for me to do." Then Dr. Carson was whisked away by the secret service.

Next, as Dr. Carson was heading back to DC, Tim and Griff were sitting in the barrel chairs at the store talking. The federal agents were now afraid to arrest them again because of the Noaans. Griff asked Tim, "What do ya think will happen next?"

Tim replied, "Yerimi told me the first thing to look out for will be a worldwide restriction placed on the internet. The Movement had to shut down all communication between the people who opposed them to move forward with their plans. Next, the media will align with the Movement by providing an unfettered conduit for their propaganda. Finally, there will be a crackdown on any individual who will not conform to the new reality. This will be done through the monetary system. Facial recognition (FR) will replace all forms of currency, allowing the Movement to control who can buy and sell.

The Movement incorporated a particular group of companies in the United States in 1989 that now process every non-cash transaction in the world. They also own the patents to the smart chips in our credit cards and to the facial recognition (FR) technology utilized by every government on the planet. Their FR system began testing in London in the nineties. Today, through social media, they now have a ninety-eight percent complete database of the world's adult population and almost all children. As a result, they have positioned themselves to totally replace our currency with our face.

This, nevertheless, is not the biblical mark of the beast. However, it is the means to enforce the mark by identifying whether or not someone is permitted to buy or sell. According to scripture, the mark of the beast is applied to all who are not sealed by the Spirit of God. Therefore, all who grieve the Holy Spirit, by ignoring His prompting to accept Yahshua, will indeed receive the mark.

The mark will be placed on the lost, the day when the worldwide law to destroy God's people is enacted. Therefore, all those who choose to support or at least accept the new world government and its religion will receive the mark."

A little confused, Griff asked, "Then what does it mean to have the mark placed in your forehead or in your hand?" Tim explained, "The best example I can think of can be illustrated by the pope's recent visit to the USA. Millions of people treated him as a deity, bowing, kissing his ring, singing praises as the motorcade passed by, and asking for his blessing. Most of these people were there because they believed in him, but many praised him because they accepted it as something they must do to get along. Still, both groups offered their worship to a man who proclaims himself to be the earthly representation of

Christ. Those who truly believe him to be what he claims will receive the mark in their foreheads and those who just go along to get along, in their hand."

Griff asked, "Well, how in the heck are people supposed to find all this out? What if someone never hears the truth?" Tim stated, "First, we tell them. Then they tell others, and the others tell others until there is no one left to tell. Imagine how many people must have viewed the broadcast from Noa? Billions have seen it, and many of them have already shared what they've seen with others. We can trust that God will see that His truth will be preached to all mankind. He works best through our weaknesses."

The two men shared a few more stories, then Griff invited Tim to stay with him and Melanie as long as he needed. They concluded their conversation with a prayer for the Noaans for all the people in leadership, especially for Dr. Carson heading into a hornet's nest of politicians in Washington, DC. Griff locked up the store, and the two men walked across the bridge to his house.

MEANWHILE IN DC

Ben had been in quiet meditation the entire flight to DC. When he arrived at the airport, the secret service agents said that President Trump wanted to see him at the White House as soon as possible. How to explain to Donald Trump why he said what he said? This is the thought that was continually haunting him until he remembered a text that said, "Do not worry when they bring you before kings, what you must say, for it will be given you." At that moment, Ben was at peace, even when he arrived at the White House, and no one would make eye contact with him.

As he entered the oval office, the President shouted, "Ben…What the hell were you thinking? Do you have any idea of the insanity you have unleashed on this town?   I thought I was the most hated man in the country. Well, I'm glad to inform you that's no longer true. I don't even know where to start. Would you please explain what happened in that damn cave that caused the most intelligent man I know to lose his ever lovin mind?"

With a level of confidence that even he didn't understand, Ben replied, "Mr. President, the Noaans specifically requested that I attend this gathering because of my extensive study and understanding of biblical prophecy. Therefore, per their request and your orders, I went to Noa to represent the United States. However, at these meetings, detailed information came to light which was undeniable.

In the broadcasts by Tim Phan, every unbelievable thing we had watched over the past three months is absolutely true. The Noaans have been attempting to teach us how to save everyone from complete and utter annihilation. Their solution is the only true solution."

Then Trump barked, "What makes you think we can trust them?" Ben answered, "Because if they wanted to harm us, there is no way we could stop them. Leo BarSet told me himself that they have no intention of defending themselves militarily, even though they have every expectation of being attacked and eventually destroyed by those they are trying to save."

"That makes no sense." Trump angrily points out, "Why would they not defend themselves?" "Why would we kill those who are trying to save us?" Ben responded. "Mr. President, either you or the person that follows you in this office will initiate America's participation into a one-world government which will be responsible for the destruction of the Noaans and lead the world into chaos." Then President Trump said, "Ben, the world is teetering on the edge, and we cannot afford to rock the boat at this time. So I have to ask you to resign to save what's left of my administration." Ben just said, "I understand, Mr. President, and I will continue to pray for you." Then Ben was quietly directed out through the back, service entrance and taken to his home.

Next, President Trump called for a special summit of world leaders, which was to be held at an abandoned airbase in Wyoming. The meeting was set up in the main hanger, converted to an extreme, off-grid site. Because of the Noaans' ability to tap into any form of technology, this site was entirely disconnected from everything. No computers, recording equipment, or communication devices of any kind were allowed beyond the outer parameter. Even the lighting and fans to cool the dignitaries were powered by a battery bank charged offsite. This was as low-tech as they could make it.

The summit started out with Trump looking for a way to coexist with the Noaans and for solutions to the problems that they had been warned about. Even so, the meeting quickly broke down into a global lynch mob, with the Noaans being found guilty of crimes against humanity.   Except for the US, England, and Japan, there was overwhelming support to call for an unconditional surrender of all Noaans and their territories. President Trump declared, "This is madness! We don't have the authority, means, or reason to prosecute the Noaans. And what makes you think they would comply anyway."

With great vehemence, the German Chancellor shouted, "Then we must appoint a confederation of nations that would have the authority! We must also pledge to give them the support needed to enforce their decisions. I mean, look at us. This meeting is being held in hiding, in this dilapidated building, because we cannot discuss these things out loud in our own offices.

Furthermore, the Noaans have admitted to attacking the security and sovereignty of every nation on earth for hundreds of years. They have already made prisoners of us all!" A thunderous roar went up from the leaders of almost every country present. President Trump responded, "The United States of America will not relinquish our authority to any confederation as long as I am President!" And the summit was adjourned. It was now clear that President Trump was not to be long for the oval office.

Two years later, following the Trump presidency, the next administration, having religious and political ties to the Movement, took the oath of office and quickly started implementing their agenda for the United States. The sweeping changes encompassed every one of the Movement's global aspirations and quickly rendered what remained of the US Constitution obsolete. With the demise of the Constitution, the US promptly merged into the new World Confederation of Nations (WCN). Furthermore, the US took its place as the military arm of the WCN to enforce the newly approved peace initiatives as the Vatican unselfishly agreed to provide the executive leadership for the confederation. The Movement had finally managed to infiltrate the protestant Christian churches and convince them that Rome was no longer the inquisition church.

THE W.C.N.

Once America had joined the Confederation, most other governments fell in line with the new order. The two major holdouts were Russia and China, who quickly capitulated when they were financially isolated by the rest of the world, causing their own populations to threaten revolution. Initially, the Confederation's changes were minimal and seemed positive for all people groups, but they became more and more intrusive as time went by.

First, all cash was replaced with specific alpha-numeric identification codes referenced by facial recognition. The digitizing of each individual's facial features effectively limited organized crime by making it almost impossible to launder the profits from illegal transactions. It also seamlessly converted currencies, thus eliminating the cost and difficulty of settling international transactions. What's more, it sped up checkout lines, as well as reduced robberies and other violent crimes. On the other hand, each transaction could be tracked and had to be approved by the Confederation.

Second, the political process was made more efficient by the top-down assignment of regional, national and local leaders. This eliminated the fraud and waste of elections, which too often didn't reflect the voter's intentions anyway. The implementation of these policies was warmly welcomed, especially by the leadership of the former communist governments, as long as they were to be the ones in charge.

Next, the World News Organization (WNO) was tasked with disseminating information to the masses through the internet. According to the WCN Parliament, this would streamline communications. They also assumed the editorial control and security of the web. This would allow the regional and local news agencies to upload news stories for approval and worldwide distribution. However, every post would have to be reviewed before being released to the web.

Finally, the Confederation unified all religions under one spiritual leader, the Pope. He was the obvious choice because Pope Francis was the most widely accepted religious figure globally. And combining all religions into one would end thousands of years of wars and destruction propagated by religious zealots. This new world religion encompassed all faiths, allowing them their own customs and ceremonies, as long as they respected everyone's right to worship in their own way and the leadership of the Pope.

At this time, those who supported the new one-world government came to be called the Citizens. They were the ones that made it their mission to suppress and eliminate any resistance to the globalization efforts of the Movement. This included any dissidents who wouldn't submit to the 'Articles of Faith and Community,' as the Vatican and the new Confederation Parliament ordained.

Considered the most grievous of these dissidents, those who held on to the archaic beliefs, there was only one standard of truth and proclaimed that there was only one way to God. This belief was offensive to the Movement and caused violent uprisings among the people. This form of verbal terrorism was not tolerated and was firmly dealt with either by the government or an assigned group of local Code Enforcers.

In a further effort to dehumanize the people of God, the Movement coined the phrase TPOGs and referred to them as radical terrorists. The Enforcer's justice for any TPOG was swift and severe. What's more, the TPOGs living in the cities were brutally being exterminated by independent gangs, as well as Code Enforcers who collected bounties on every TPOG captured dead or alive. Adding insult to injury, the WNO reported these murderous attacks as uprisings by the TPOGs, which provoked the populous to call out all the more for their destruction.

Due to the non-stop news coverage about the violence supposedly caused by the TPOGs, the main topic of interest of the Hollywood elites was the atrocities perpetrated by the Christians. Who, according to the talking heads, were calling themselves TPOGs and revolting against the peace initiatives of the Confederation.

However, a few started to question the reports because they didn't make sense. Tom and Rita Banks, for instance. They had personally seen much of the violence in San Francisco and LA, but the conflicts they witnessed were one-sided, with the Christians being on the receiving end of the violence.

But whatever the facts, Tom and Rita decided to go up to their retreat near Aspen to wait until things got back to normal. However, when they arrived at the main house, they found it occupied by the District Satrap, the local magistrate assigned by the Confederation. The Satrap's name was Richard Burns, who used to be the Deputy Mayor of Aspen. His duties were to judge and pass sentences on the TPOGs, brought in from all over the Aspen district.

When Tom protested that this was an illegal seizure of his property, Richard reminded him that they were no longer living under the US Constitution and confiscated property according to Confederation guidelines.   He did, however, say they could stay in the guest house if they wished. Tom didn't want to press the issue because he and Rita were surrounded by a dozen heavily armed men. So they went to the guesthouse and started unpacking.

Both Tom and Rita were unusually quiet as they settled into the guesthouse until Rita said, "Tom, I'm scared. I never imagined that the one world order, which we championed, would turn out like this." Then Tom said, "I have put my time, money, and celebrity into this…Utopia, which has turned out to be worse than Germany in the 1930s. Dammit! The worst part is I knew better! I'm going to go take a look around to see what's going on here." Rita looked worried, so Tom assured her, "I'll be careful."

As Tom stepped onto the front porch, he heard shotguns being fired about a quarter of a mile away towards the western overlook, so he decided to casually stroll down the path in that direction. When he was almost to the overlook, another volley of gunfire startled him. Stepping out of the woods, he found twelve very young men talking and laughing while reloading their shotguns.

"How's the hunting?" Tom asked. The one in charge said, "Pretty good. Hey, aren't you Tom Banks?" Tom smiled and said. "Last time I looked...Now what you guys shootin at?" Another one of the men pointed over the bluff and said, "TPOGs." Tom walked up to the edge and looked down into the woods, two hundred feet below. There were hundreds of bloodied bodies scattered among the trees and piled up on the ground, at the bottom of the cliff.

He remembered that he was taught the last-day prophecies in Sunday school as a child. The predictions were frightening to him at the time, but if not for those lessons, he would not have grasped what was happening now, right before his eyes. Then gathering his thoughts, he composed himself and calling upon his many years of acting experience, he coldly said, "Well, I better go see if Rita has us unpacked yet. Good work, gentlemen." He turned and headed back up the path.

Tom made it nearly halfway back before he had to stop. He looked to make sure no one was around, then stepped off the path and sat down on a rock with his head in his hands. He was crying and wondering how he came to be in this place at this time. And what happened to that boy who asked Jesus to come into his heart so many years ago. Just then, part of a memory verse he hadn't thought of in fifty years came into his mind, "I stand at the door and knock..." Sitting on that rock, Tom reopened that door and remembered that he had been made a new creature at age thirteen. The courage of a lion filled his heart, and he was no longer afraid, so he headed back to the guesthouse to talk with Rita.

He decided to take the long way around, where he found the stables surrounded by armed guards. The building was very large with forty full-size stables and an indoor warmup area. Tom walked up to one of the guards and asked him, "What are you guarding in there, Fort Knox?" The guard said smugly, "Just a bunch of TPOGs, about seventy of em. We're supposed to get another shipment in the mornin, so we've been clearin em out all day, tryin to make some room." Tom asked as if he didn't know, "What do you do with them?" The guard answered, "We take em, ten at a time, to Satrap Burns. He pronounces sentence on them, and then we take them to the bluff, to be executed." Tom asked, "How many more are you expecting?" "Probably another two hundred or so. This is supposed to be all that's left in this district. It'll take three to four days to take care of them all." "Well, I'd better be getting back. See ya." Tom said as he turned and walked away.

When he arrived back at the guesthouse, he found Rita terrified, and she said, "I heard gunshots, a lot of them. What are they shooting?" Tom answered, "I'm afraid they've turned our home into Auschwitz. They are executing hundreds of men, women, and children at the overlook, dropping their bodies into the woods below."

Horrified, Rita asked, "Why?" Then in a hushed voice, Tom told her, "Because they're Christians, just because they are Christians…Rita, I am a Christian too." Since when?" She probed. Tom then told her all about giving his heart to Jesus when he was just thirteen and then renewing his relationship, just now in the woods. Then Tom said, "Someone has to speak for these people; we can't leave it like this. We will go back to LA tomorrow and talk to everyone who will listen."

So, Tom and Rita lay in bed all night, talking and making plans. In the morning, they didn't even load the car back up. They got in and started down the gravel drive but were stopped at the gate by six armed men who told them that Satrap Burns wanted to talk to them before they went into town. Tom said they would drop by the main house as soon as they got back, but the men insisted.

As they pulled back up to the main house, they saw Richard standing on the front porch. Tom got out of the car and asked him what was so important that it couldn't wait until they got back? Richard told Rita and Tom that he had recording devices strategically placed throughout the guesthouse, and he had recorded their discussions from the night before. As they were speaking, three guards walked up from behind and loaded a round into the chambers of their weapons. Richard ordered, "Put them with the others!" Tom hysterically shouted. "Have you lost your mind? You can't do this to us!" Suddenly, one of the guards hit Tom in the face with the butt of his gun. Richard turned and slowly walked back into the house. Then two other guards forced Tom and Rita to walk to the stables at gunpoint.

Rita and Tom were thrown into a stall with a family of four and two elderly gentlemen who helped to stop Tom's head from bleeding. A couple of hours later, they heard Richard Burns shout from the porch, "They're all guilty, carry out sentence immediately!" Rita asked Tom, "What are we going to do?" The two old men were praying until they heard this, and the one named Bob asked them, "Have you ever asked Jesus to forgive for your sins?"

Tom nodded yes, but Rita said, "I don't know. How do I do it?" Bob said, "Jesus is the incarnation of God, His only begotten Son who lived a perfect life, died on a cross, and rose from the dead to forgive us our sins. God has promised that if we accept His forgiveness in the name of Jesus, we will be saved. Repeat after me as I pray. Dear Heavenly Father...forgive me for my sins...in the name of Jesus Christ, your Son...Amen! That's it. If you prayed that prayer and meant it, then you are saved!" Rita said, "I don't know how I know, but I know in my heart that I am saved!" Then Tom and Rita fell into each other's arms tearfully, praising the Lord for His mercy.

Just seconds later, the gate flew open, and the guard barked. "Get this first group up to the bluffs." They were led away along with a group from the next stall, down the path to the overlook. When they arrived, the same young men were there, and they were surprised to see the Banks in the group of TPOGs. One of the executioners asked, "What happened? Did ya find Jesus since you left yesterday? Tom smiled and answered, "Well, yes. Yes, I did.

The youngest of the executioners got out of line, walked up to Tom, and asked sternly, "Do you really think Jesus is going to forgive your sins?" Tom answered confidently, "I really do." The young man's expression softened, and he asked Tom quietly, "Do you think he would forgive me?" Taken back, Tom answered again, "I really do."

Finally, with everyone watching and wondering what he was doing, the young man walked back over to the line of men, laid down his shotgun, took off his ammo vest, and went back to the line of TPOGs and stood by Tom. The head of the detail hollered, "Just what the hell do you think you're doing?" He said with tears in his eyes, "I'm going with them." For the first time in fifty years, Tom felt the joy of knowing that he would stand before God forgiven, and even though he had wasted most of his life, he would not show up empty-handed.

BACK IN RELIANCE AGAIN

Before long, the same persecution had spread to most of the cities worldwide. Therefore, refugees flooded out of the most populated areas into the countryside, wilderness, or wastelands searching for safety. Many of the Christians in the rural areas offered the little they had to ease their suffering. Also, at this time, Griff and Melanie were struggling to provide for the nearly two hundred men, women, and children who had fled to Reliance.

Reliance and many other sanctuaries received support with shipments of food and medicine from Noa. Sada and two younger Noaans, Randolph and Ronald, made daily trips to Reliance from Noa. Randolph and Ronald were fifty-two-year-old twins whose mom was a big fan of Randolph Scott and Ronald Reagan. They were chosen to help Sada because they were young, strong, and extremely fast runners.

However, as the group swelled to over three hundred, it became too much, so Sada told Griff that they would have to relocate the refugees to Noa. It was getting far too dangerous and difficult to transport such large amounts of food and supplies. Therefore, the following day the group started the long and challenging trip up to the boulder which covered the elevator shaft. It took most of the day to get all three hundred and twenty-three refuges up to the rock. Noa was jamming satellite and drone signals to make them useless in finding the group as they made their trek.

When they arrived, Sada announced that the lift could only handle thirty riders at a time and that there would be a team of Noaans to assist them. So, they started with families with young children and the elderly. The remaining adults were to be the last to go. This was going to take eleven trips to transport everyone. Randolph, Ronald, and Sada would go down separately, with Sada on the last transport.

However, as Randolph and twenty-nine of the refuges prepared for the ninth trip, a huge explosion billowed out around the stone, killing everyone on the lift and destroying the MMG. The enormous stone fell back in place, shaking the whole area and killing three more refugees standing near the entranceway. Even those standing farther back were knocked to the ground by the concussion.

Sada immediately turned to look at Ronald, who had tears in his eyes as he said, "This was a bomb on one of the refuges, wasn't it?" Sada answered, "It had to be." Then Ronald asked, "Why would anyone hate us this much?" "They hate us because Yahshua loves us, and they hate Yahshua more than anything. The explosion will give away our position, so we better get these people somewhere safe. I can do this by myself if you aren't up to it right now." Ronald stood up straight and replied. "We have been preparing for this our whole life. My brother and countless others have laid down their lives to complete this mission; I will do no less."

Sada and Ronald took the fifty remaining refuges to a couple of off-grid cabins that Griff had built years before, a few miles upriver from Reliance in a narrow holler. The cabins were designed to sleep ten people each, so they could rotate who slept on the floors. Since the holler was so narrow, it made it easy for Sada to calculate when they could move freely outside without worrying about satellites spotting them. All in all, they were safe for the time being, and this time of year, they could forage for enough food to sustain themselves.

Not long after, the Confederation, with low-tech communications and on-the-ground recon essence, had located all eleven Noaan civilizations and their entrances. As a result, they had determined the most efficient plan of attack, which would enable them to neutralize all the civilizations simultaneously. The project would utilize multiple weapon systems in a specific sequence at the various entrances to the Noaan's caverns.

First, the centers of possible ground support surrounding the penetration points would be cleared by carpet bombing with MOABs and Daisy Cutters to prevent backup resistance from the sympathetic communities in the area.

Immediately following the destruction of the adjacent communities, the outer defenses shielding their elevators and light access shafts would be penetrated from the air with high impact, delayed triggered, bunker-busting bombs.

Next, the shafts will be cleared for access by dropping a high number of laser-guided, precision napalm bombs directly into the shafts from squadrons of attack helicopters.

Finally, neutron radiation and gas devices would be lowered into the chamber's main levels. Then large diaphragms would inflate in the shafts to seal them. The devices will then detonate, releasing a gas that will completely fill all the chambers in a matter of hours, killing all air-breathing animals. The structures and plant life, however, will remain unaffected. Now, all the military needed was the order to strike.

When the central council of the WCN met in the Vatican, they quickly gave unanimous approval with only one question asked by the Pope, "Will death by neutron radiation gas be humane?" The Commanding General simply answered, "Humane? No, but it will be effective, and there will be absolutely no possible chance of escape." The plan was passed, and a date was set for the incursion.

On the morning of the set date, Sada and Ronald were running a ten-mile recon essence sweep of the woods around the cabins when Sada spotted a sniper positioned on the summit of the next ridge. In just minutes, He and Ronald had quietly worked their way up behind the sniper to observe him. He didn't seem to be headed anywhere; he was just waiting for something. Sada whispered, "This ain't good!"

Next, two squadrons of attack helicopters flew down the river valley from the direction of the dam, then stopped and hovered in the center of the gorge just a few hundred feet away. Seconds later, they were overflown by a C-4 cargo plane, which continued on down the river gorge towards Reliance. When the plane neared Reliance, the rear cargo door slowly opened, and a large container parachuted downwards, directly towards the store. Sada suddenly jumped up, grabbed the sniper by his vest, and held him up with just one hand as he tossed his rifle off the cliff.

Sada was standing at the edge of the tree line, looking downriver where Reliance was transformed into a giant yellow fireball. The explosion was so powerful he could see the air, thousands of feet above the town, being blown away in every direction. In a few seconds, they heard the rumble from the blast echoing up the gorge. Then a few seconds later, Sada heard another rumble coming from the north, so he stepped out of the trees and looked towards Tellico, where he saw the same kind of blast cloud forming above it. The sanctuaries for the refugees around the entrance points to Noa were all being bombed out of existence.

When Sada's mind started to clear up, he realized that he still had the sniper dangling by his side and that he was exposed. Suddenly a severe burning in Sada's chest spun him around, and instinctively, he tossed the sniper to a safe location behind a large rock. Three more fifty-caliber sniper rounds from three other sniper positions tore through his body armor, and he fell. With his last breath, he ordered

Ronald, "RUN!" Immediately, two gunships opened fire on him, and Sada disappeared in a cloud of dust.

Ronald, knowing they would soon napalm the entire area, grabbed the sniper, tore off his ammo vest, threw him over his shoulder, and ran until he was sure they were a safe distance away. When Ronald finally stopped, he gently sat the sniper on the ground, and then to the sniper's surprise, he asked him his name. The sniper replied, "My name is Randy, Randy Lappin." Ronald hesitated for a moment and then said, "My name is Ronald. My twin brother's name was Randy. He was recently killed by a Movement suicide bomber.

Your team just killed a man named Sada BarSet, one of the best and wisest men I've ever known. The only reason I didn't leave you to burn in the napalm is that Sada's last act was to save your life, and I wasn't going to let that be in vain." Randy said softly, "But, I'm your enemy!"

Both of them turned to look south when they heard the distant sound of the bunker busters pounding the hundred-ton stone into gravel. Then Ronald said, "You're not the enemy. You just work for him. And when the sound of those bombs fades away, everyone else I know and love will be dead. I have no idea why I'm still alive, but I will do my duty to my King as long as I am. I'm going to tell you a story. When I'm done, I will send you back to your unit. I will tell you as much as you are willing to hear."

For the next two hours, Ronald told Randy about God's plan of salvation from creation up to Jesus' return. When he finished, he stood up, told Randy that he would be praying for him, then took off through the woods and was out of sight in just seconds.

Randy sat contemplating what he had been told and what would happen to him if he allowed himself to believe. He got up and headed back to his base camp, all the way telling himself that it would be foolish to become a Christian. It would be the end of everything he holds dear.

And by the time he reached camp, he had convinced himself that he didn't really believe in God. Immediately upon arriving at his base, Randy checked in with his C.O. and was debriefed by the First Sergeant with his entire platoon present.

Most of them just wanted to know what it was like to face a Noaan. On the other hand, the sergeant was more interested in the body armor and camouflage technology incorporated into the Bigfoot suit. However, one of the gunners, the one responsible for finishing Sada off, had picked up on the part of Randy's story about the plan of salvation. Later the gunner found himself praying and asking God's forgiveness for killing one of His faithful servants.

Everyone had heard exactly what they wanted to hear; some heard an exciting war story, others heard sensitive intelligence about the enemy, but only one heard the plan of salvation. The gunner remembered his grandfather telling him, "Truth is available to all who seek it, but so is foolishness, so ask God to help you seek wisely."

THE LAST OF THE LAST

After running for fifteen minutes and covering more ground than an elk could have in an hour, Ronald stopped beside a stream to catch his breath. The surface atmosphere made it difficult for him to maintain his quickest pace for extended periods without his respirator. So Ronald knelt down, bowed his head, and prayed for the strength and wisdom to do whatever God had for him to do. When Ronald opened his eyes, the woods were illuminated with a bright light. A man was standing next to him. Ronald fell with his face to the ground, but the man touched him and stood him up on his feet.

Then the man said, "I have been sent in response to your prayer, to encourage and instruct you in these final days. Know this, that you and the fifty-one souls down at the cabins, will witness the coming of the Lord in the clouds, with your own eyes." Ronald mournfully declared. "Sada, Randolph, and everyone else is gone!" The angel responded, "They are not gone. The Lord promised that all who put their faith in him would never die. They and countless others are sleeping in wait of the day when they will see Him, face to face. The Word foretold of two deaths.

The first death is a temporary state, where the breath of life returns to God, your personage is taken into God's care until the resurrection, and the physical body returns to the matter from which it was taken. Even then, the physical body hasn't completely died.

There are sub-molecule-sized particles called Sominids which function as your DNA's memory. These Sominids hold all the data needed to remake a perfect you, and they cannot be destroyed by anything on Earth.

On the other hand, the second death is described in the Word as "The wages of sin." This death is when God withdraws Himself completely from a lost soul, which results in their breath of life ceasing. At the same time, their memories and life knowledge, which made them who they were, will fade into nothingness, and they will no longer exist. This death is absolute! Blessed are those who have a part in the first resurrection, for they will never see the second death."

All of a sudden, it occurred to Ronald that the angel had said fifty-one souls, so he asked, "Fifty-one souls? Sada and I left only fifty people at the cabins. Who's the fifty-first?" "Tim Phan." The angel answered, "Griff had sent him up to the cabins to check on the refuges when the attack came.

Nevertheless, you need to hurry back down there. They are all scared and confused, so tell them that there is nothing to fear and hold on a little longer. Not one will be lost. Now go!" The angel disappeared, and Ronald felt his strength renewed as he raced, faster than ever through the thick green Appalachian woodlands.

In the meantime, the Movement, fully knowing that the Earth's last days were at hand, refused to relent in their tireless persecution of the TPOGs. With mindless disobedience to God, the Movement committed all their resources to their destruction.

The WCN had an emergency session at the Vatican because of an impending disaster of their own making. One of which was an effort to balance the world's environment by introducing deadly pathogens into some of Africa's and South America's food shipments to reduce the world's population to what they had determined to be a sustainable level. However, the pathogens mutated and became airborne, spreading throughout Asia, Australia, and beyond.

What's more, many of the major cities had deteriorated into anarchy, as the governments lost their ability to provide essential services, which affected sanitation, then utilities, and finally food supplies. Many people stayed in their homes, hoping the government would come to their rescue, but others formed rogue militias and took whatever they wanted. As for the governments, they watched helplessly as their militaries and police departments were disintegrating.

With the catastrophic failure of their policies, the leadership of the WCN was now in panic mode. Knowing that they would be blamed, they decided to deflect the responsibility for the plagues to the TOPGs, claiming they were acts of biological terrorism. This type of distraction has often been used to shift the responsibility for the death and destruction that plagued a population away from those in power. Since the days long before Nero, governments have blamed God's people for the troubles which had come upon their nations. This time, however, it was the whole world!

And as long as their populations were chasing TPOGs, the WCN leadership would be safe. Therefore, in an effort to gain some time, the WCN Parliament ordered that all TPOGs be hunted down and exterminated for the safety and security of the nations.

In the meantime, the WCN leadership started barricading themselves, along with the world's elite and as many people as it would take to maintain their lifestyle, in the chambers once occupied by the Noaans. Hopefully, this would protect them from the calamities occurring on the surface.

It had been just a few years since Brian's time in the bunker, and now the sixth millennium was coming to a climactic close. Wars were on every continent as the new One World Government attempted to enforce their new laws and subjected the so-called dissidents to death and imprisonment. The world, therefore, had been reduced to just two camps, the Movement and The People of God.

By this time, the Noaans had been all but extinguished. The TPOGs retreated to the last remaining wildernesses and mountain sanctuaries, with the Movement hounding their every step. Even so, in a last-ditch effort, some of them stayed behind, knowing they had the only solution for the dying world! They were met with unimaginable persecution, all for the hope that just one would listen.

Just recently, many of God's people had attempted to store up food, water, clothing, and even weapons in preparation for the last days. However, it was all in vain. There was no way to prepare for what was happening other than sharing the Message. As prophesied, everything in this world was going to be destroyed except for those who put their faith in God's grace by accepting His salvation through His Son, Jesus Christ!

The enemy had instilled fear into the hearts of the masses. Even many of those who professed to be Christian succumbed to the terror. Those who had trusted in their own works to save them. This was the time when by laying down your life, you saved it, and by saving your life, you lost it forever! The Bible tells us, it is appointed for all men to die once, but only the lost will see the second death. This is why the TPOGs tried so desperately to warn all those who were lost.

The TPOG's Message was that we are all sinners, and there is nothing we can do apart from God's grace to be saved. We are all wretched, miserable, poor, blind, and naked, and without Jesus' righteousness to clothe us, we cannot stand before God! Even so, few listened, and fewer were willing to believe.

The remaining believers found themselves under assault spiritually as well. Knowing that he was running out of time, the enemy pounded their senses with guilt, doubt, and condemnation. He told them that they had put their faith in a fairy tale, and it was not enough to save them.

Insanity is the only way to describe his state of mind, as he realized the fear of facing his Creator and God in the judgment!

The TPOGs knew that time was running out, and all this was going to end! Up until this time, the Movement had persecuted the Christians unto death. But the WCN had no idea that when they finally passed the law calling for the immediate worldwide destruction of all TPOGs, they had sealed their own fate and simultaneously sealed the fate of all unsaved persons with the mark of the beast.

The Christians, however, had been expecting this because Yahshua revealed it to them almost two thousand years before that all who were called by His name would face tribulation. In John 16:33, He said, *"These things I have spoken unto you, that in me ye might have peace. In the world ye shall have tribulation: but be of good cheer; I have overcome the world."* Tribulation is the evil that mankind can inflict upon man. But Yahshua also told them that all who are sealed by His Spirit will be spared God's wrath. Therefore, all those who received the mark of the beast will suffer the full wrath of God poured out without mercy.

The Movement quickly realized that their every effort was failing them! When the WCN tried to cut off the TPOGs food and water supplies, their own economies crashed, their crops dried up, and they blew away. The great Vatican City, thought to be the seat of all power, fell in one night to the very ones it had deceived. They burned the city and its inhabitants with fire and tore down its walls. The Pope, however, had escaped, only to find that there was nowhere for him to run. The heads of governments worldwide sat in terror, knowing the same fate was coming for them and that their gods, their riches, and their power could not save them.

Millions began attempting suicide without success and ended up mangled and in horrible pain, but they couldn't die. In the same way, they had treated the TPOGs, they were being made to wait their turn.

Around the world, the skies opened up as giant hailstones fell, destroying buildings, sinking great ships, and killing nearly everything outdoors. Next, an enormous comet penetrated the atmosphere, and as the outer portion was burned up, it filled the sky with toxic red dust, which encircled the planet and poisoned a third of the world's water supplies. This catastrophe alone killed billions and caused most survivors to break out in boils all over their bodies. Another result of the comet was the powered metal flakes that circulated throughout the atmosphere, amplified the effects of the sun's rays, and made it impossible to go outside without protection.

Meanwhile, back in the Hiwassee River gorge, a few miles north of where Reliance used to be, some of the refugees were weeding the vegetable garden, others were thatching the roofs, and the rest had a bible study on the front porch of the large cabin.

God had covered them with his hand of protection, just as the angel told Ronald months before. They had seen the red skies and knew from the prophecies in the book of Revelation what was going on in the rest of the world. They also knew that there were others like themselves in the same situation, which was a sign that their deliverance was near. Ronald walked over to the porch and bowed his head while Tim had the closing prayer. After a few seconds of silence, a powerful baritone voice broke out in song. It was Ronald, and he was singing, "Soon and very soon, we are going to see the King…." Everyone joined in, totally unafraid of being heard, as their voices rang out God's praises down the valley.

As they finished the song, they realized that something profound had just happened. The reddish-gray skies had fled away, and a shimmering gold brightness had taken their place. The brightness seemed to fill the whole sky and show a great light worldwide. There was no night or darkness anywhere.

All those who were lost on the earth feared the light greatly. Some tried to escape from it, and others tried to fight against it. The few surviving generals marshaled their troops, planes, and missile batteries to unleash every weapon of war against the light.

With everyone at the cabin looking up into the sky, they didn't notice the young family of five that walked up from the direction of Reliance. When Ronald spotted them, he was flabbergasted! "Where did you come from?" he asked.

Through his tears, the young father told him, "I asked the Lord for just one thing before I died, that I could tell someone who loved the Noaan, I killed on the mountain near here, how sorry I was.

My name is Bill, and I am so sorry." At first, Ronald couldn't speak, then he said, "I think you can tell him yourself in just a few minutes. How did you know where to come?" Bill said. "The Lord led me to come to Reliance, then we just followed the singing." Ronald quietly asked, "What about Randy?" Bill just shook his head no.

Then the ground began to shake as the entire universe thundered with a voice that proclaimed, "It is done! All who are Clean, are Clean, all who are Unclean, shall remain Unclean!" Then the Earth was moved out of its place as if it was trying to resist God's will by attempting to hold back His treasure. Nevertheless, as the lost desperately ran to hide from Him, the ground erupted, and the seas exploded! God's treasure, the saved who had died throughout all ages, burst forth and faster than the speed of light found themselves in His presence, above the sky...

THE REST OF THE STORY

...Suddenly standing, looking at his hands and feeling the blood pulse through his veins, Brian Gregory wonders. Is this it? Am I really here? Will God accept me? As he becomes aware of the multitude of people and angels around him, he realizes that he can feel their emotions and understand their thoughts. When he and the others started making eye contact, a singular thought suddenly flashed in their minds...Jesus!

Then Brian, and all the others, as if they were one, pivoted and saw Him! The first thing Brian noticed was that He was smiling with a Joy that only He could have. As He radiated Love from Himself, all their guilt melted away, and He replaced their fears with His own indescribable Joy! The people of God actually started glowing! However, the light shone brightest around the children!

The countless children who had died throughout the ages. All those who had not lived to reach the age of choice. Babies were carried to their mother's arms by the awestruck angels. The little ones whose parents had chosen not to come became the children of those who had none of their own. Finally, the light grew brighter than the sun as many of the women felt life returning to their womb, and they burst out in tears of joy! This was the beginning of the Healing of the Nations.

At that moment, with just a glance, Yahshua sent His angels to recover the remainder of His treasure. His remaining treasure were those who had not perished in the persecution. The angels are amazing creatures, more beautiful than anything on earth. They shot straight upwards over the heads of the saints and, with hyper-precision, raced downward towards the Earth like bolts of lightning.

All at once, the narrow holler around Griff's cabins glowed as fifty-seven angels appeared, each taking the hand of one of the survivors and then shot upwards at the speed of thought. Ronald and the others found themselves standing in the middle of a great congregation of saints and angels above the sky. And there was Yahshua!

In less than a heartbeat, the surviving saints of God were standing among us. As they were figuring out the same thing we had only seconds earlier, their Joy became complete as well. God's work was almost done. Finally, He bestowed his greatest gift on His children...Eternal Life!

The children of God who were now made whole broke out in song, which God had put into their hearts at creation...a song He had waited all this time to hear. As the song went up, rows and rows of angels encircled them. The angels could not sing this song themselves, so they folded their wings and bowed their heads in worship to God for His amazing power and Love. Because what God had started so long ago, He had now finished.

Brian thought that there was no way for his joy to increase because his family, his friends, including Mel and Dave, Mr. Paulson, and Mr. Lynn, were all standing beside him! There were even two ex-scientists standing there with arms raised in praise for the undeserved Grace of God.

Then, Brian saw the Noaans with the red hem of the martyrs on their robes. And there was Sada, smiling as if to say, I told you so! Brian ran over, grabbed him, and gave him a huge bear hug. Life was at last complete because God is Love!

Brian remembered back when he had visited some of the churches where he heard preachers saying that God was angry and was coming to destroy the wicked! However, this was not so! He came to save the wicked from their sin, the same sin that would eventually kill the world. This was a rescue mission!

God gave them the Word, the evidence of their faith and Himself to die. Thus, He paid the price for their redemption! As a result, all those who came to Him in faith, He made clean; those who did not did so by their own choice. "In Him was life; and the life was the light of men. And the light shineth in darkness; and the darkness comprehended it not."

Far below, the world grew cold, dark, and lifeless, except for the one who had rebelled in Heaven and was condemned to wander the Earth alone until the day of his final judgment. Even the stars withheld their light as all life animating energy faded from every living creature. Soon, there was nothing alive on earth, no plants, no animals, and no people; only the enemy remained. He was spiritually chained to this planet, forced to walk among the corpses for a thousand years.

The unbearable brightness the lost had seen radiated from Yahshua's perfect righteousness.   And the darkness that came upon the earth was simply a result of Him turning away his face. This had nothing to do with those who chose not to come. It was only about those who came. It had only and always been about them from creation to the cross to now.

Brian was just beginning to understand when suddenly, they all found themselves standing on the sea of glass in the Kingdom itself! The only thing Sada could say was, "WOW!" Brian smiled and told him, "What do you know? I am Bigfoot!

The arrival in the Kingdom was amazing. Their new bodies were unbelievable works of art...Mansions. None of them could remember the moment they changed because it took only a microsecond. Which was kind of odd because they could recall every microsecond since then with clarity and detail. Ten seconds in these bodies, with these minds, would've been more than enough, but Yahshua had given them eternity, a piece of Himself.

Choose wisely...Be There!

G.B. Miller